# EPICALLY
## Earnest

# EPICALLY

*Earnest*

## BY MOLLY HORAN

CLARION BOOKS
An Imprint of *HarperCollins*Publishers

Clarion Books is an imprint of HarperCollins Publishers.

Epically Earnest

Copyright © 2022 by Molly Horan

All rights reserved. Printed in the United States of America. No part of this book
may be used or reproduced in any manner whatsoever without written permission
except in the case of brief quotations embodied in critical articles and reviews. For
information address HarperCollins Children's Books, a division of HarperCollins
Publishers, 195 Broadway, New York, NY 10007.

www.epicreads.com

ISBN 978-0-35-856613-7

Typography by Samira Iravani
22 23 24 25 26  PC/LSCC  10 9 8 7 6 5 4 3 2 1

First Edition

To my dad. For everything.

# CHAPTER ONE

**The truth is rarely pure and never simple.**

—OSCAR WILDE, *THE IMPORTANCE OF BEING EARNEST*

> So, don't kill me, but I stole your spit.

This was the text I got in the lobby of Algie's apartment complex, from Algie himself, who I knew had just been informed of my arrival by Mark, the night doorman. Algie likes to send texts right before actually greeting people, "to set the tone." But I suspected this particular text was his half-hearted attempt to mitigate my anger by dropping the bomb while we were still separated by thirty-six floors. Normally he's good at making me forget whatever genuinely enraging thing he's done now. It's possible the little effort he needs to put into getting my near instant forgiveness makes me kind of a doormat. Taking my spit against my express wishes, however, crossed a line and I felt a little vindicated by the fact Algie knew that.

When I reached the penthouse, Algie was leaning against the doorframe wearing a top hat with the brim tipped over his eyes, an already-open can of Diet Sunkist in his hand, a totally inadequate peace offering. He didn't look up when the elevator dinged, but instead said, in his best English accent, "Beverage, madam?"

"You're going to try to be cute? That's your plan—ply me with orange soda and Algernon charm I've built up a tolerance to for the last decade? I could call the cops, you know," I said, stomping past him into his apartment, past the floor-to-ceiling Impressionist paintings, past a life-size replica of the Venus de Milo, and into his room, where I sat on the very edge of his four-poster bed (an honest-to-god set piece from an off-Broadway production of *Scrooge*), making sure to telepathize that I could leave at any second.

"And what, Janey, would you charge me with? If spit theft was a crime, I would have been in juvie since the first grade."

"Shut up, there was no spit theft either way between you and Brett A."

"Maybe not Brett A., but Mitch H.—"

"How have you never had mono?"

"Strength of character."

"You stole my spit."

"For your own good—"

"Transporting samples of bodily autonomy across state lines is probably a crime."

"When you make up crimes, at least make them grammatically correct."

"Algie! You know I don't want to know, I've told you I don't. This is a complete violation of—"

I faltered—tired of talking, tired of arguing—suddenly hit by a wave of bone-deep exhaustion I hadn't felt since I ran the mile with a 102-degree fever (in my defense, I always feel like I'm going to die when I run the mile, so I didn't really notice a difference). I flopped onto the refrigerator-size teddy bear Algie got from whatever guy was following him around in a lovesick haze last Valentine's Day.

I felt Algie's head rest gently on my back, a sign of just how much trouble he knew he was in with me — normally he flung his body onto mine with absolutely no consideration of the damage his elbows could do to my kidneys.

"Don't you want to know what I found?" he asked in a whisper, a register I was pretty sure I'd only heard from him on the stage when he was playing someone capable of being quiet.

"That I'm mostly Western European, slightly Eastern European, with probably one percent something that seems totally random because genetic testing you got a Groupon for probably isn't as scientific as you'd like it to be?" I asked.

"Janey, I found a familial match."

I was going to throw up. Hopefully on Algie. No, I was going to pass out. Or possibly become the Incredible Hulk. None of the emotions or sensations flowing through me were matching up with anything I'd ever felt before.

Somehow, I got out, in a death rasp, "Well, Mr. *St. Vincent High School Register* editor in chief, way to bury the fucking lede."

———

My legal name is Jane Worthing, but that's not the name on my original birth certificate, wherever that is. You might know me as the Bag

Baby, which various sites on the internet have described as "one of the first viral videos of the twenty-first century." I'd like to say I'm honored to be a part of such an important milestone in web culture. But instead, I tend to get hung up on the fact that one or more of my birth parents left me, in an oversize Gucci handbag in the back of the Poughkeepsie train station. What separates me from other unfortunate infants who have been abandoned in far-less infant-friendly locales and haven't reached a fraction of my view count is my dad. Of course, in that moment he hadn't quite claimed the dad mantle, but he did have his unique way with words. My soon-to-be aunt was the one who captured the moment on her flip phone as Dad cautiously approached the bag (instead of calling security like you're supposed to do when something in a train station looks suspicious).

"Careful, Mickey, you don't know what's in there. Could be one of those coppah heads, like that lady from Dahchester found in her toilet" you can hear my aunt say in her thick-as-hot-fudge-in-the-fridge Boston accent.

If all of life's a stage, this is the opening line of the play that is Jane Worthing. Dad keeps slowly electric sliding up to the bag until, out of nowhere, up pops my one-year-old head, little blonde pigtails flopping everywhere, big cheeked, blue eyed, with an expression that clearly says, "Whoever woke me up from my nap is about to get *fucked up*," but, you know, cuter. And then Dad says it, the line immortalized in late-night monologues, an SNL sketch, and a hand-drawn caricature sent to us by the guy who draws the *Zits* cartoon. "Jesus, Anne, people are leavin' their babies everywhere these days." Which, if you think about it (and I have, a lot), is pretty flippant for someone who was about to fight so intensely to become my legal guardian.

"Once I picked you out of that god-awful ugly thing, that was that," Dad always said when I would ask what lead a single, twenty-something, self-professed dude-bro (once I explained what that was) to adopt an unclaimed toddler. "I swear, Janey, it didn't even occur to me you were going to be such a chick magnet!"

So, after a search for anyone who was missing a toddler and a lot of vetting and paperwork, Dad officially adopted me. I don't really remember Dad's days as a single parent (though they did yield some pretty amusing photos of what he thought a toddler should wear) because my magical woman-attracting powers worked — he married Mom before my fourth birthday. So really, I've had a pretty average, normal childhood, if you just ignore the first four years. And I did, most of the time. Did I sometimes in the middle of the night wonder who abandoned me, and why, and if there was anyone out there who could explain how I got the vaguely bird-shaped scar on my ankle or if kiwi allergies run in my birth family? Sure. But it doesn't help anything to wonder about mysteries that might never be answered. Have you ever noticed that the historians who are still looking for Amelia Earhart always seem kind of on edge? I think it's because if a mystery is big enough and old enough, you have to worry that the answer might not be big enough to fill the hole the question has carved in you.

This is only one reason why I'd avoided all the ways I could go full twenty-first-century Nancy Drew and 23andMe my way into some kind of teary family reunion on a morning show. Because that's what would happen if I put out any kind of message onto any corner of the internet. Some bored blogger would pick it up, then it's a *HuffPo* headline, then I have sixty-seven cousins who have all been offered round-trip airfare to the *Today* show to explain that they always wondered what became of that cute toddler their forgetful aunt used to keep in an oversize tote.

There is no way I could have a private moment with any recovered family members if I asked the internet for help. All the internet people would demand their nationally televised Hallmark moment, and I'd never know if this collection of strangers with my eyes really wanted to get to know me or just wanted to visit LA. It was a decision my parents respected. It was a decision Algie mostly respected. But then DNA kit companies started advertising on every true crime podcast Algie constantly listened to. Once he understood family secrets were just a drop of drool away, he became obsessed with me getting one. Even though I'd told him no, texted him no, and spelled it out in carrot sticks during a particularly boring Netflix binge, he hadn't listened. And now, because Algie never listens, I had a familial match. I didn't want a familial match. My family is my dad and my mom and all the aunts and uncles and cousins who have populated my Christmases and summer vacations. But it's basically impossible to ignore a question once the answer seems just within reach — it's out there. Attention has been called to it. I still think Eve might have never eaten the apple if God was just like, "And here's a bunch of basic trees, now moving on to everything else in this literal paradise."

"It's a first cousin," Algie said as I sat up. A first cousin. Their parent is the sibling of my bio parent. My head started swimming again. That seemed too close, like too much information right away. Spit-service stories I had read during long nights of procrastination all found second cousins or third stepcousins twice removed to be starting points that could be investigated further, or not. A first cousin is practically the end of the story. Family tree fully formed.

"Have you . . . ?" I asked, too nervous to complete the question.

"I didn't click into the tree. I didn't want to see it before you."

I smiled a little, despite my still-simmering anger. There was nothing Algie would love more than to discover the answer to a seventeen-year-old mystery before me, or anyone else, but knowing he didn't proceed without me made me feel a little more open to forgiving him before graduation. Algie had been trying to convince me to track down my birth parents for as long as I could remember. Whenever he pushed it, I tried to remind myself that his curiosity came from equal parts excitement about living in close proximity to an honest-to-god mystery and his love for me. I knew that whenever he sensed some kind of emotional defense, which was usually just me not wanting to make a fool of myself (or not wanting to fool around in a public place), he thought it was because there was some kind of gaping hole in my heart carved by whoever gifted me a few chromosomes then left me behind.

"It doesn't matter. Someone, or some people, didn't want me, but my parents did. I actually think a bigger chunk of the population would have healthy family relationships if we were more willing to reorganize when the ones we were born into, or you know, produced, don't quite seem to fit."

"I really can't wait for you to run for office someday on the baby abandonment platform."

"Give me your laptop."

And there it was: a brown acorn, artfully perched on the name of my blood relative, Sandra Snoot. Oh god, I hoped that wasn't my last name. My first last name. I put the curser over it, wishing the act of clicking it would make more noise to allow this very momentous moment to seem more, well, cinematically momentous.

"You don't have to do anything with it, you know. I can even take you to this amazing hypnotist downtown who can probably remove this entire afternoon from your memory," Algie said, taking my non–track pad hand and squeezing it.

"I am Jane Worthing, and who I was my first year can't change that," I said, like it was a mantra I'd had all my life instead of something I had just come up with. I clicked.

Family trees are pretty straight forward, but my eyes seemed to take in nothing as I manically scanned the cartoon oak suddenly taking up the screen. I closed my eyes and took a few deep breaths, trying to steady myself, or remember how to read, or both.

I found Sandra's branch: parents Steven Snoot and Emily Tennen. I let my eyes slide to the left of Steven. One brother, b. 1979, d. 1988. Not my birth father. I looked at Emily's branch. Only child. My brain felt like it was full of rusty gears, moving and turning, but not quite latching on to what it needed to make sense of what I was seeing.

"Her mom's name, Emily. It's in gray. That means she was adopted," Algie said, pointing at the screen.

"Oh. Well. That's that, then," I said. I knew it didn't have to be, of course. It was possible Emily had done some detective work of her own, that she'd found birth parents and biological siblings, that she had once met a bio sister or brother who had a new baby girl, who she hadn't been in touch with since. I could message Sandra. I could track down Emily's contact info. I could take a trip to New Jersey; it wasn't like I had any big spring break plans anyway. But Emily's gray name felt like a sign. The universe had given me an amazing family, and I worried I might offend it if I tried to work out what happened before. And I actually had a lot of respect for the universe. I didn't want to find out what happens when you offend it.

"Are you sure?" Algie asked.

The last thing I remembered being one hundred percent sure of was my decision to get the purple big-kid bike with the pink streamers instead of the lime-green one with the yellow basket when I was seven. But I nodded anyway. I really wanted to be sure.

---

I assumed it was lingering shame that made Algie wait three episodes and two boxes of Pop-Tarts to bring up Cecil, my cousin who had moved to Brooklyn from Boston earlier this month, suddenly placing him in Algie's orbit. After a very, very brief introduction at my house, Algie had DMed him, Cecil messaged back, they chatted, and now my little baby cousin was destined to become just another notch on Algie's bedpost — which, let me remind you, he had four of.

"So, Janey, what do you think I should get Cecil for his birthday? I was thinking a book of poetry, but that is a little overdone. Do you think he'd appreciate a book of my poetry, or is that a little too DIY?"

I was pretty sure that if Algie wrote him a haiku on a Post-it Note, Cecil would start writing their wedding vows. I wasn't going to tell Algie that.

"Seriously, Algie, he's so little —"

"He's almost sixteen."

"But for the next week he's only fifteen —"

"And I am seventeen, and Zac Efron was eighteen when he starred in *High School Musical*. Why are we listing age facts?"

"He's just so much less experienced than you, it would be like setting up a middle schooler with, I don't know, James Deen."

"The actor?"

"The porn star."

"That makes more sense. You can't hear the different spelling. Definitely not the breakfast sausage guy, though?"

"That's Jimmy Dean."

"Right."

"Your ability to banter in the face of my genuine concern for my family makes me feel so much better about introducing you two," I said narrowing my eyes for emphasis.

"Introducing us! I have no idea what kind of dark-web voodoo you pulled off to make sure we were never so much as suggested to each other on any platform, but 'They met through a mutual friend after years of said friend deliberately keeping them apart' is not a great start to a Modern Love column."

I groaned as I rolled over on my back, staring at the ceiling. Cecil and Algie were the only two people under thirty who religiously read Modern Love, which should have given me more hope in their potential as a couple. But I also knew that Cecil liked to hum "Someday My Prince Will Come" under his breath as he read, while Algie liked to tell me about the latest piece of evidence that the sheeple still believe humans are capable of monogamy. I tried to brainstorm texts to gently warn Cecil away from Algie as I looked at the words scribbled in Sharpie just to the left of Algie's chandelier: "Algie was here, and continues to be here, and expects to remain here for the foreseeable future." And then "Janey was here, and will be here periodically."

"You know, just because I pretend to sleep through some of the trash rom-coms you insist on watching doesn't mean I haven't gotten something out of them through osmosis. Maybe this is the classic, clichéd story of the hopeless romantic thawing the heart of the cynic! Cecil might be the only one who can make me be a better man. Like the girl in *A Walk to Remember*."

"She dies of cancer," I reminded him. I could practically hear his smirk in response.

"This conversation is going nowhere. Conversations about my love life are so boring. Will I get the guy? Yes. No suspense! It's time to turn to someone with a struggle. Someone who has watched the one they love across a crowded cell phone screen for too many years."

"Why do you sound like you're pitching a Netflix show right now?"

"You know my pilot isn't ready to pitch yet. Stop quipping, I'm trying to give you good news. Gwen's coming over for spring break. Staying for the week, actually."

"Gwen, like, your cousin Gwen?" I asked, which is as stupid as asking, "Oprah, like Oprah Winfrey, Oprah?" There was only one Gwen in my life—Algie's cousin. Gwen had basically single-handedly caused my sexual awakening at age thirteen, when she showed up to Algie's pool party in a black bikini, bright red lip gloss, and the kind of confidence every other middle school girl in the world has to fake. I spent that whole afternoon cursing my chlorine-faded one piece, my lack of a pedicure, and the two square inches of stubble I'd somehow missed on my thighs. I'd arrived at the pool that day pale, reasonably carefree, and solidly heterosexual. I left it the light rose of organic strawberry ice cream, lovesick, and totally bi.

For two years after that fateful day, our interactions were limited to Algie's birthday parties and the most carefully crafted Instagram comments I had ever written under her posts sharing her life at a gorgeous Connecticut prep school. But sophomore year we'd discovered a mutual love of this queer fantasy show, *Rings of Saturn*, that I'd been convinced no one watched but me. This meant that on Tuesday nights, I watched the most poignant portrayal of intergalactic sapphic love ever aired on cable TV and texted Gwen a series of reaction GIFs to capture my thoughts. Her texts were so funny and smart and insightful, it made me want to print them out and send them to anyone who's written a think piece about how communication is being killed by Gen Z and our rapidly texting fingers. But simultaneous swooning is not the same thing as being in the same room with a person. And while I like to think of myself as a fairly capable human being, I will admit that getting within a five-foot range of Gwen did kind of leave me significantly more awkward than usual.

Still, the thought of her in such close proximity for a week had my imagination humming—pictures of things that had not happened, but suddenly seemed possible, flashed through my mind like a flip-book wielded by a kid on sugar. Gwen, in a lacy slip that she wore as daywear because she could totally pull it off, offering to teach me how to do a cat's eye. Gwen getting ready for bed, unrolling a sleeping bag that happened to be right next to my sleeping bag on the floor of Algie's den, drowsily asking me big life questions. I imagined she'd whisper after a particularly insightful response from me, "Wow, Janey, you just— You get it." Gwen putting her hand on mine while we watched a movie, our fingers interlacing, her perfectly manicured nail stroking my thumb to the beat of the music in the background, and I'd realize she notices movie scores too. And just as the strings swell and the hero saves the day, I kiss her, hard, insistent, and—

"Stop. Janey. You have fanfic face. I wholly support the make-out sessions that will someday lead to your legal entry into the Moncrieff family, but I don't want you imagining doing my cousin while lying on my bear. What would Dear Abby say?"

"So, is Gwen, like, I mean, I haven't seen that guy, what's his face, in any of her pictures lately, right?" I asked, aiming for casual. It had taken all of my willpower not to ask her myself.

"Smooth, Janey. No, Gwen is currently a free agent. I'm afraid her last suitor wasn't quite up to my aunt's standards for her one and only daughter."

I'd never actually met Gwen's mom, but I knew she's the kind of person who can seem intimidating from a photo—it's not just that every hair is in place, every tiny stitched logo aligned just so. It's something in her eyes. I avoided the family photos in Algie's house just so I wouldn't have to be under her judgy stare, even for a moment.

"Wasn't he, like, captain of the football team and got into Harvard early decision?" I asked.

"You sure know a lot about someone you call what's his face. Yes, he was the all-American boy, just as Arthur Miller would have written him and just as beautiful and chiseled as Ryan Murphy would have cast. But he didn't check that elusive quality my dear aunt insists upon for anyone who poses for prom pictures with her Gweny."

"Which is?" I asked.

"A pedigree. A family tree that money actually does grow on. Albums that are full of generations of barons and titans and other people who wear ascots and monocles and canes. What's his name is apparently the son of a start-up CEO, who is the son of someone who was still paying off his very reasonable mortgage when he died. She won't rest until her daughter marries into a dynasty," Algie said.

"But Gwen is eighteen. And this isn't Victorian England. What does it matter who she dates when she's, like, statistically a decade away from even getting engaged?" I asked.

"Janey, when I understand my aunt, or my family, or fellow rich people, you will be the first person I invite to my TED Talk. Maybe she just wants to get Gwen in the habit of going out with What's His Face the Third. Maybe she's hoping Gwen could fall hopelessly in love with a Carnegie and elope over the summer so she won't have to pay Gwen's college tuition. I don't know. I'm sure she'll explain it all in her memoir someday."

I continued to stare at the ceiling, considering this fun new wrinkle in my yearslong romantic daydream. All the moisturizing masks and articles on how to be a sparkling conversationalist wouldn't change the fact that not only did I lack an illustrious family legacy, I lacked any knowledge of my biological family legacy period. And I wasn't sure if I was ready to go looking for it.

"Do you think she would accept someone with some moderate internet fame instead?" I asked.

"That's an interesting question, Janey. If fame, in the twenty-first century, is the most valuable commodity, if followers equal influence and influence equals power, which in turn equals money, would my aunt be okay with you sticking your tongue down her daughter's throat? Very interesting question," he said, thoughtfully stroking his chin. I tried to throw the giant teddy bear at him, but I wasn't strong enough, so I instead pitched a pillow with the word *Slut* written across it in sequins at his face. He caught it one-handed and put it gently on his bed, smoothing the sequins.

"I know you don't care about my happiness, Algie, and I know you don't get having a crush for longer than a week, but I really . . . like her," I trailed off. It seemed like such a childish thing to say, almost like a whine. And what I felt about Gwen was more than the crush I developed when I would still, on special occasions, stuff socks in my bra. She got all my references. She understood why Lizbeth couldn't be with Raquel, no matter how the rabid shippers tried to push them on the rest of us. I thought, I mean I was pretty sure, she might actually understand me.

"Janey, you know that I love you. I gave up the chance to hook up with Hemsworth-esque crew-team members when you were in your time of need."

"You can't take credit for comforting me after a mess that you created," I groaned.

"But I want to be clear: it wasn't guilt that took me out of those perfectly chiseled arms. It was love."

The incident he was referring to, another event I'd gotten really good at not thinking about, was Bag Baby Babe.

I had made it through most of my life with minimal reminders of my five minutes of fame. There were some Bag Baby taunts on the bus in middle school, but they were quickly quashed by Algie. I had almost come to think of it as just a weird baby story, the kind everyone has that might get brought up at family reunions or in group texts. Then last summer, one month before the start of senior year and one week after my eighteenth birthday Algie commented on a glamour shot of us on Instagram, coining what he thought was the ingenious hashtag #BagBabyBabe. It was supposed to be funny, and a compliment, and something seen only by my 514 Instagram followers. But someone who saw it and connected Bag Baby to my Instagram account shared it on Reddit and Tumblr. From there it was found by someone on MyWebFeed who did just enough digging to confirm I was the Bag Baby, and of legal age to receive the full wrath of trolls, before posting the original video and the Instagram pic with the headline BAG BABY BABE: SHE'S LEAVING HER BOOBIES EVERYWHERE THESE DAYS.

I am not a crier. I didn't cry when Mary Stevenson broke up with me the day before homecoming freshman year. I screamed but did not shed a tear when I dropped a bowling ball on my foot at Alice Riley's sweet sixteen, even though I broke three toes. But as I scrolled through pages one and two and three of strangers talking about my face and my chest and the various things they'd like to do to both, I sobbed. I cried until I felt dehydrated, until Dad had called every police station in the State of New York, asking who was going to do something about HungHunk55 sexually harassing his teenage daughter, until Mom was all cried out and Algie had stopped sending me pics of his own tear-streaked face, all captioned simply "I'm so so sorry." And sometime after I had reached the point of becoming a shriveled-up raisin of a person, Algie had come over with milkshakes and promises to watch whatever I wanted for as long as I wanted. Even though I was not going to let him off the hook at that moment, I did feel completely loved and taken care of, though shaken with the knowledge that the people who loved me could ultimately not protect me.

"You know if I could take back Bag Baby Babe, I would," Algie said.

I stayed silent.

"But right now, what we should be focusing on isn't the past, and isn't the distant future when you might have to stare down the stand-in for every socialite caricature ever and the full force of my aunt's generations-strong snobbery. Before you worry about winning over Gwen's mother, you should probably be focused on actually winning over Gwen. Doing that out of order would be weird. Like, creepy weird," Algie said.

"Fine, Algie, fine. I very temporarily, like for the next five minutes, put my fate in your hands. What should I do?"

"You should not think about it. Don't think about Gwen, don't obsess about what you're going to say or do, just make your mind blank, the only thing in your cerebrum should be little brain tumbleweeds. When you obsess, you get a really intense expression in your eyes and you lose all control of how loud you talk, and those two things are serious mood killers. Think about things unrelated to Gwen, and then, when you're finally alone together, be yourself. I mean, definitely censor yourself a little. But the general shape of yourself," Algie said.

I flipped onto my stomach and shoved my face into the teddy bear's. Don't obsess. Be myself. That sounded easy enough, in theory. In actuality, I was already making a mental list of interesting conversation starters and wondering if I started watching tutorials now, whether I'd be able to perfect my waterfall braid before spring break.

# CHAPTER TWO

**The very essence of romance is uncertainty.**

−OSCAR WILDE, *THE IMPORTANCE OF BEING EARNEST*

The obsessing was still going strong at five a.m. the Friday before spring break. I was debating whether or not I should go to bed or start a sixth "Cute Cats Lolz" YouTube playlist when my Skype icon started bouncing and a window popped up to inform me Cecil was also not worried about the fact a mere three hours separated us from first period. Clicking into the call filled my laptop screen with Cecil, his forehead smothered in what looked like blueberry yogurt, wearing a T-shirt that read, SAVE THE WHALES, SAVE OURSELVES.

"C, you missed your mouth a little there," I said, gesturing to his lumpy forehead. His grin sent cracks through the blue mass.

"It's an organic pore-shrinking mask. The jar says if you use it every day for six months, your pores disappear, like, one hundred percent."

"I'm pretty sure you need your pores. If they were really the spleen of the skin, celebrities definitely would have figured out how to remove them by now," I pointed out, taking a quick look in the tiny, hazy corner square to see just how visible mine were. "I can always ice them in the morning. I'm getting my senior pictures taken tomorrow.

I want to look my best," he said, running his fingers through his three inches of curly black hair.

"But you're a sophomore."

"I know. I want to have a practice run. They're important!"

"Plus, you know they airbrush school photos, right? Have you never looked at a yearbook? Everyone looks like they just got microdermabrasion."

Cecil looked concerned for a moment but quickly recovered, the new smile sending a whole chunk of the mask sliding down his face.

"Well, I'm just lightening the retouch dude's workload. I'll be famous at the photo place, the first kid who didn't need Photoshop!"

I let him vamp for a sec, wondering if the ability to turn anything remotely negative into a gleaming positive is an inherited trait. When we were ten and eight, watching *Bambi* for the first time, he noticed I was crying and solemnly said, "If his mother didn't die, he wouldn't have become Bambi, you know?" as he offered me the rest of his shark gummies.

"Janey, do you believe in love at first sight? Or, actually, fate? And also, that a certain kind of magnetic force that is evenly distributed through your blood stream lies dormant most of the time, but when you meet the right person, is activated, until you're slowly pulled closer and closer, bit by bit, helpless against a magnetic force bigger than you and every plan you've ever made?"

"So Algie's still texting you?"

The little bits of face I could see through the mask turned red.

"He's just so . . . I mean, I thought I got him, and then he'll text me this totally brilliant thing, and I'll be like, *I don't get him, but god, I want to get him.*"

"He's really not that complicated, C."

"He is! He's just this beautiful kaleidoscope and I keep twisting and twisting, and every new shift makes him even more dazzling."

I really didn't want to burst out laughing while Cecil was baring his soul, but all I could picture was the myriad of truly filthy jokes Algie would riff off of C's kaleidoscope metaphor.

The thing I've realized about people this far down the rabbit hole of a crush is they become level-ten optimists in the face of any warning signs. Seriously, I once told my friend Sarah that the fellow camp counselor she had been going after all summer had tipsily confessed at the bonfire that he was secretly dating a different girl at all four of our sister camps, and she just softy whispered, "I love multitaskers." Still, I felt like I had to at least try to warn Cecil.

"Cecil, Algie . . . Algie is not someone you should probably . . ." I was desperately reaching for a way to cockblock my cousin, which really made me wish I had gone to bed when my eyes started screaming at me around one a.m.

"Algie is kind of a man whore" was what I decided on, even though it wasn't really keeping with my New Year's resolution to avoid any slut-shaming in my day-to-day life. There's just not a more concise way to tell my cousin who's still waiting for his Mr. Darcy that Algie is more like Mr. Wickham. But, like, a Mr. Wickham with the technology to call and invite over a hot guy from bio or soccer four to five nights a week, depending on his parents' business schedules.

"God, Janey, I'm going to be sixteen in a week. You're not that much older than me. I know stuff. I've seen stuff," Cecil huffed, absentmindedly picking a blueberry out of his eyebrow.

I felt fairly confident that the only stuff Cecil had seen was on his cell phone, using more than his fair share of his family's data plan. But I could see streaks of daylight coming in through my bedroom window, and if I hoped to get even an hour of sleep before being asked to conjugate something, I figured I shouldn't broach the topic of Cecil's porn habits.

"I know, I know. You're old. So old and wise, by tomorrow you'll have to give up on the pore purge and start stealing your mom's anti-aging serum," I said smiling, offering a silent truce.

"I know you're saying it as a joke, but all the blogs I read say you should start an antiaging regimen by the time you hit eighteen," he said, looking so painfully earnest I wanted to reach through the screen and give him a hug.

"I guess I'll need to fit a run to Sephora somewhere into my schedule today then. I've been letting my skin get old for months now. Good night, Cecil. Just, be careful with Algie, will you?" I said in a sleepy, last-ditch effort to protect Cecil's heart, which I realized was driven from about fifty percent protective older cousin and fifty percent self-interest — I didn't think I could live in a world where Cecil Cardew became jaded.

He kept smiling even as he rolled his eyes.

"I can handle myself, Janey. And by the way, I've set Andy up with both his girlfriends, and I'm pretty sure he and Casey are going to be together literally forever. You're supposed to help your best friend find love, not scare off the people who might be interested. Or, you know, definitely are interested. Anyway, good night!" He ended the call, leaving me staring at my wallpaper. It was a photo of Algie and me taken just after junior prom, him in his top hat, tails, and Converse ("Being stylish doesn't mean I shouldn't pay homage to the decades of prom renegades before me, Janey") and me in the ball gown from the national tour of *Cinderella*.

Algie had purchased the dress at a Broadway charity auction and presented it to me when he picked me up for school one morning like he had just grabbed me a latte on his way to first period. What wasn't in the photo: Algie's date, Phil Denir, a sweet junior whose eyes turned into cartoon hearts whenever Algie walked into a room. Algie ditched him seven songs in to make out behind the hall with a senior from St. Marks who'd also come with someone else. Also not in the picture: my date, Abby Cadmic, my friend since first-grade tap class, who'd I'd gone with platonically. She'd refused to speak to me for the entire summer because Phil is her stepbrother and I had refused to ice out Algie for his admittedly very dickish behavior. Maybe I should have iced Algie out for it. Maybe I should have iced Algie out for a lot of things. I lay down on the floor and spread my arms and legs out, starfish style, the only position where I could get any decent thinking done (so many term papers had been drafted while staring at an aging spider splat on the ceiling). Algie was not a bad person, I had always reasoned; Algie was a bad boyfriend. Lots of people are a bad "blank" without that badness coloring the entirety of their person. Some unfortunate hopefuls on reality shows with the nicest backstories are bad singers, but seem like good people.

Of course, it's possible I should have been troubled by the fact I needed to go into starfish mode to reason out why my best friend was a good person. If I was really being honest with myself, which I normally tried to avoid, I'd have to admit I always assumed Algie going through guys with an assembly-line kind of efficiency was a phase. That pretty soon he'd look behind him and say, "Holy shit, in this particular aspect of my life, I'm a monster," and spend the rest of his life as the kind of sweet and selfless boyfriend who sometimes gets profiled by the *Huffington Post* for their devotion.

And there was no reason Cecil couldn't be the guy who would, as Algie had said, sarcastically or not, "thaw the heart of the cynic." I could have told Cecil about all the parts of Algie that I loved. Like how he donated almost all his outrageous monthly allowance to schools in danger of losing their theater funding because, he said, too much time spent alone with your show tunes playlist leads to madness. Or how because I don't know what my actual, literal birth date is (Dad picked August 7 in honor of some old basketball player), Algie will sometimes drop a cupcake with a candle next to my lunch "just in case." Or how sometimes when we get to see an actual Broadway show, he grips my hand at a moment that isn't particularly scary or even emotional, and I know it's because in that moment he's just so terrified that it will never be him up there.

But then I think of poor Phil, and how he looked for the rest of the summer — like that deflated girl in the old anti-pot PSA they showed us in health class. I wanted to believe Algie would be Dr. Jekyll with Cecil and we'd all be able to hang out together until I eventually acted as a dual maid of honor–best woman for their wedding. But I knew that once a first date had been set, Algie would go full Mr. Hyde.

I sat up just enough to grab my cell off the desk, then lay back down. I considered the phone, then put it on my stomach, watching it rise and fall with each breath I took. I wondered why I didn't mention to Cecil that I had another cousin. And aunt. Another cousin and aunt who could potentially lead me to even more new family members. Or why I didn't mention it to my parents when I got in from Algie's place. Or why I hadn't posed any related questions to the Magic 8 Ball that had been getting me through big life decisions since the yearbook-staff-or-spring-play quandary of eighth grade.

When I closed my eyes, I saw that stupid cartoon acorn getting bigger and bigger, ready to explode and rain down all sorts of relations on me. Uncles and second cousins and third cousins once removed. My phone's rise and fall stopped for a moment as that idea paralyzed me. My daydream siblings had changed over the years, evolving in basically lockstep with whatever movie I was watching at the time, meaning either (a) I had an almost criminal lack of imagination or (b) couching my dreams in fictional characters made them seem just unreal enough that I wouldn't have to share any sense of loss or long-ing with my parents.

When I was really little, juice-boxes-and-animal-crackers little, I dreamed of a small-classroom–size group of siblings, like in *Cheaper by the Dozen*, imagining where I might fit into a cluster large enough for everyone to have a clear, comfortable designation: the jock, the rebel, the science geek, the girly girl, the baby. Then Algie introduced me to A Series of Unfortunate Events, and I pictured my mystery siblings as the missing pieces of a team, thinking that once we found each other, I'd discover I had some incredible talent that worked in tandem with theirs and would make us the best elementary school detectives/coders/filmmakers in the country.

Sandra Snoot. It sounded so made up. Maybe it was made up. I suddenly sat bolt upright, my phone sliding off my stomach and clattering to the floor. A series of extreme privacy settings compounded by the internet's general attention span of a goldfish meant that the Bag Baby trolls hadn't really bothered me in months beyond a few extremely nasty comments on a homecoming article I published in *The Register*. But maybe one of the 4chan bros who had been so offended when I didn't take them up on their motorboating offer was attempting to catfish me. Would it really have been so hard to hijack my results and create a fake cousin and a conveniently dead-end aunt to make me think finding my bio family might actually be possible? That was probably it. That had to be it. What could I, or Algie, or LetsOpenUpThisFamilialWound.com find that the private investigator my parents hired when I was a toddler hadn't? How could there be hope when I had been told by the two people who loved me more than anything in the world that the door to any hope was pretty much slammed shut? I picked up my phone, typed *Sandra Snoot* into Google, and instantly received what seemed like an increasingly desperate list from the search engine bot.

"Did you mean . . . Did you mean . . . Did you mean . . . Surely you know that Sandra Snoot is a made-up name, so you meant something else" Google seemed to say when it came back with exactly zero results. And if Google can't find you, you don't exist. Just to prove my point, I searched my own name, and scrolled through page after page of thumbnails of Gucci bags and blonde pigtails and my father in enormous, ripped cargo pants. It wasn't until the middle of the fifth page that links to my social media and articles for the school paper came up, along with a link to a blog covering Astoria that had taken a photo of me circa second grade. I'm standing in front of the Ferris wheel at our neighborhood spring carnival, holding my father's hand, grinning at my mother as she offers me her cotton candy. It could be a stock photo for a family. You just know that anyone looking at that photo would see a girl who doesn't need to be asking any questions about where she belongs.

I'm findable. It just sits with me, heavy at the base of my neck, that the real parts — the parts that describe who I am, and who I love, and who loves me — come up after the bag articles. I wonder what to make of the difference between interesting and intimate.

# CHAPTER THREE

*Education is an admirable thing, but it is well to remember
from time to time that nothing that is worth knowing
can be taught.*

—OSCAR WILDE

The Friday before any school break always seems ridiculous and fake, but the Friday before the last break of all of high school is a complete joke. We had our acceptance letters. We'd learned everything we were going to learn for our AP tests before hitting the kind of brain saturation that makes calc formulas and treaty dates spill out of your ears. But still, they had our diplomas, which I imagined were kept in a chest, like a giant version of the cardboard ones filled with congratulatory stickers from elementary school. Those sheets of paper were the sum total of every scratch-and-sniff YOU'RE GRAPE! sticker we had ever earned on a math test, and to get the diplomas, we had to trek through the halls for another five weeks. But that didn't mean I was going to trek in real pants.

The student body and the teachers, principals, and other adults who could potentially write us up for dress code violations had come to an agreement last spring. We promised, as a collective of everyone from the dweebies to the sportos, that no girl would bare the hint of a shoulder or an inch of stomach and no guy would even think of lowering his shorts to expose his boxers, if we could all come to class in our pajamas. The administration seemed to think it was safer for us to be fuzzy and frumpy rather than risk an orgy breaking out at lunch if three or more girls happened to come to school in tank tops. My wardrobe since then had mostly consisted of various combinations of flannel, fleece, and Henleys. I kind of figured I could sort out my look in college.

*"Jan-EEEE"* I heard my father bellow from downstairs, with the same tonality of a football bro calling another football bro from across the hall.

I bounded down the stairs, three at a time, hoping my mother wouldn't appear to inform me that this particular habit would leave me with shattered ankles. Every day I made a little promise to myself that I almost always kept — *This will be the stupidest thing I do today.*

Dad was standing by my chair with a giant grin on his face, making sure I watched as a giant green disc slid from his battered non-stick pan onto my plate. He then put his arms up in a position of athletic victory, Pam still sizzling in the pan held high above his head.

"What have you done to that pancake?" I asked, unwilling to sit down since that would bring me even closer to the crime against breakfast.

"Pancake? Would I serve my only daughter a pancake, full of refined sugar and gluten, when I could serve her a paleo cake full of the same ingredients our ancestors ate for centuries?" Dad asked, finally lowering the pan as Mom came out of the living room eying the pancake like it was a bug she hadn't quite decided if she should squash or spare.

"There's one Pop-Tart left, Janey," she said, squeezing my shoulder before she sat down next to me, opening the paper to her favorite section, the obituaries. I ignored Dad's groan as I fished a slightly smushed blueberry Pop-Tart out of the pantry. I plopped down next to Mom again, peeking over her shoulder at a sea of smiling, elderly faces that might have been charming if their presence at my breakfast table weren't a stark reminder of my own mortality.

"Ma, couldn't you just read the police blotter like a normal person?" I asked, with a mouth full of violently blue dye.

"We're all gonna die, Janey. But these people lived good lives. People miss them and love them enough to sit down and write a nice little note to them that they'll never actually read. The obits are the happiest section of the paper. Go ahead, see what your dad's reading. What's on the front page of the *Gazette* that would pair better with my toast?" Mom asked.

Dad, who was holding my surprisingly rigid rejected pancake in one hand and the bottle of maple syrup in the other, glanced down at the front page.

"'Fire Destroys Apartment Complex,'" Dad read, nodding to Mom then to me, the gesture meant to acknowledge that Mom had a point.

I grabbed my backpack from the counter and swung it on in one of my more graceful moments, pausing for an eye roll before leaning into Mom for a hug.

"Is your morbidness just a yearslong hint that I better deliver with your eventual obit?" I asked.

"I know you'll make me proud, Janey. Just remember, I'll add a month of haunting for every typo."

What my mom didn't know was that I'd been practicing. She'd been reading the obits at the breakfast table for as long as I could remember. And for just about as long, sharing the breakfast table with strangers who had been loved, but were gone, made me want to cry into my Cap'n Crunch. So when I started taking a creative writing class freshman year, I started writing my living obits, or, as I think of them, obits with all that morbidity magically erased. They included all the accomplishments and nice things collected in obits that would seem so much brighter if they weren't in the shadow of actual death. I'd written them for my parents, friends, classmates, teachers, our nice mailman who always leaves Halloween candy, the busker on the L train who sings these amazing original songs and then always gives any money she earns to the first homeless person who comes on the train next. I even have some for my bio parents. Actually, I have a lot for my bio parents. You have more creative options when you have fewer facts to work with. But Mom's was the first one I ever wrote:

---

MAGGIE CHRISTINE WORTHING, LOVING
MOTHER, INCREDIBLE LIBRARIAN

Maggie Christine Worthing was born in 1973 in a small town
in Maine that had exactly zero bookstores, zero Targets

that also sold books, and zero libraries not connected to a church. After going through nearly every volume her church had to offer (and, as she would often explain to her own daughter, learning more about the intricacies of beheadings than any eighth-grader should), she began a school-wide, then town-wide campaign to have a community library built. She would eventually become the Walnut Creek Memorial Library's first page. Moving to New York to get her master's in library science, she met a young single father, Mickey Worthing, and his two-year-old daughter, Jane. They were married two years later. Maggie is always remembered, in the way you can still remember those who aren't dead, as the kind of librarian who will recall not just that you like horror novels, but that you like horror novels that happen to take place in old cowboy ghost towns. She has started so many special programs to make sure every reader knows they're welcome that patrons have sometimes assumed that a blank space on the event calendar meant the library would be closed. Her husband and daughter will often find books on their bedside tables with Post-it Notes directing them to certain passages, always with the message "Made me think of you!" Maggie Worthing could (and still can, because again, she is not dead) make you feel understood.

---

Like most things about him, Algie's car was ridiculous, expensive, and had somehow grown on me. For his sixteenth birthday, his parents had presented him with something appropriately shiny and red, with a tiny animal trying to throw itself from the hood like it could sense that every mile the car went was killing more of its habitat. Algie, ever the gracious son of the one percent, thanked his parents, and post-party politely asked if he could exchange it for something more him. Within a week he had bought a completely refurbished 1972 Volkswagen bus, painted jet black, with the back modeled after Gwyneth Paltrow's living room. When I pointed out he had all the style of a kidnapper, he countered, "Sometimes form must be sacrificed for function, and I intend to function at the highest form on and off the road."

Sometimes Algie sounded like a riddle you read off a popsicle stick, but that's easy to overlook when you can eat lunch every day inside a bus that's so decked out it would be Goop-approved. The thing was so monstrous, it took up multiple spaces on Algie's good parking days. But since he was one of, like, four students who actually had a car, the teachers rarely wrote him up for taking more than his fair share of parking lot real estate.

As I grabbed the few books I'd forgotten to pack up last night, I could see that Algie had texted me a single GIF of E.T.'s disembodied finger, which never ceased to be creepy out of context, no matter how many times he used it to announce he's "right here." His bus was parked in the driveway, and I could see he was rocking his aging professor look—black-rimmed glasses with no glass, a tweed jacket with elbow patches, and a black bowtie. I assumed it was meant to be ironic — a studious outfit for a day of watching whatever DVDs our teachers forgot to take home after winter break.

I was about to compliment him as I slid into the passenger seat when I felt a hand on my shoulder and I released a string of swears and nonsense words at a pitch that could have shattered glass.

I whipped around to see what demonic spirit was chilling in the back, but was greeted by something far more frightening: Gwen, looking completely perfect in lilac skinny jeans and a matching tank top, her dark brown hair piled on top of her head with just a few curly wisps framing her face like a real-life Disney princess's. And she was actually smiling at me, in my shapeless fleece pajama pants and an old band shirt from freshman year I had thought was extremely witty at the time reading PERCUSSION KNOWS HOW TO BANG.

"Sorry for sneaking up on you. I guess Algie didn't tell you I'm taking a little field trip to public school today?" Gwen asked.

She said *public* like it was both horrifying and fascinating, which was so snobby and rude, but then she smiled again, and I became totally willing to overlook any and all classist comments. I considered pointing out that we had to test into it since it was the second-best public school in the entirety of New York City, or talking up our Apple store–level computer lab, but I figured the oppressive smell of burnt tater tots that hits you as soon as you set foot in the building would undo any of my hype. I was just grateful she hadn't said anything about having to come all the way into Queens to pick me up, as my outer-borough pride was strong, and easily wounded.

"I don't know that there's much to see today. I think it's long-dog day in the caf, so that can be an experience. Sometimes the dorkier freshman will use them as swords," I said, already in a shame spiral at my immediate use of phallic imagery.

"And I'm pretty sure Ms. B. is close enough to retirement that she'll finally let Cody play *Silence of the Lambs*. Watching the greatest cannibal film of all time while being stared down by cutouts of all the presidents is an experience I doubt you get at Excelsior Academy for Future Real Housewives," Algie said, finally pulling out of the driveway.

"Actually, Algernon, Excelsior has only produced Bachelorettes and one regrettable contestant on *Naked and Afraid*," Gwen said.

"A statistic I'm sure is at the very front of the brochure," Algie said, grinning.

"Of course. Right next to the Venn diagram of alumni who became senators, alumni who married senators, and alumni who had all social and political aspirations dashed by a leaked sex tape."

"You Excelsior girls sure are classy."

"That's what I have second period: Grace and Class. After calc, but before How to Convince Your Parents That Your Prom Date Is the Kind of Guy Who Always, Always Wears a Power Suit."

I could feel my stomach ice over at Gwen's mention of her junior prom date — I had seen the photos on Instagram last spring, Gwen's waist encircled by the strong forearm of what's his face. So I shifted to a safer subject — *Rings of Saturn*.

"You know, I read that they're thinking about making a full-on, coming-to-a-theater-near-you movie for *Saturn*," I said. I had in fact read a dubious tweet from a fan site, but I was desperate to salvage my part of this conversation.

"Can you imagine seeing Antoni on the big screen? Or Roxy? Or Layla? God, the casting director will have to be a genius to get the chemistry just right," Gwen said with a kind of half sigh.

"No one's getting a MacArthur genius grant for finding hot people," Algie said, pulling into one of the few student spots.

"But finding hot people who will still be hot even when they're covered in purple body paint and sometimes have little spikes growing out of their heads? I think that takes some level of talent," I said.

"You could do it, Janey. You always find the Easter eggs in *Saturn*. You have a good eye," Gwen said, as she grabbed her purse and hopped out of the bus.

Gwen thought I had a good eye. This was going to be a very good day, even if it was at public school.

We walked to the front door together with Algie singsonging, "We're here, dear cousin. And just remember, if you have any plans to shout, 'Let them eat cake,' be prepared to back that up — a slice of factory-grade Funfetti will run you two fifty-five, and I don't think our lunch ladies take Amex."

Gwen answered by flipping him off, then put on a pair of heart-shaped purple plastic sunglasses. I could feel my good eyes morphing into hearts in response. I shook my head a little, as if trying to dislodge any witty thoughts that had gotten trapped in one of the more crowded lobes.

We separated at the door of my first-period, AP English class and Algie shepherded Gwen to his advanced Latin class. Today, in honor of spring break, they would be watching a copy of *The Rocky Horror Picture Show* his teacher had captioned in Latin. I waved a sad goodbye as I headed inside to my desk. I knew we'd be watching *Romeo and Juliet* — the old one. Not the Leo one. Not even the one that came out in our actual lifetime, but the one my mom remembers watching in her English class. Because even if Ms. Lydia understood it was her God-given right not to make up a lesson plan for a pre-break Friday, it didn't mean she wanted us to get any potential enjoyment from one of our eighty-seven-minute sessions with her. I swear to god, Ms. L. had some kind of heinous, *Carrie*-style stuff pulled on her in high school. But instead of getting revenge on her actual peers, she realized she had the power to make multiple generations of high schoolers suffer.

I took my seat, the best one I'd managed to score in my entire high school career: back left corner, close to the door, in a kind of florescent-light blind spot that meant little to no chance of being caught with an early-morning snack. It was also right beside Raina, possibly the best person to have as a seatmate. She tried to top herself almost every day with a Wes Anderson–esque commitment to whimsy. Today, she had dressed herself in a bubble gum–pink tennis dress, matching platform sneakers with tightly coiled, spring-like laces, and tiny pink teddy bear heads dangling from her ears that gently hit her jaw when she turned her head. Every few minutes she'd blow a perfectly even, perfectly spherical giant pink bubble.

"Hey, Raina."

She nodded, gently, so as not to disturb her bubble before it popped with a satisfying crack. She spit the pink glob into a wrapper, then put the balled-up wrapper into what I guessed had been an Altoids tin before she had decoupaged it with vintage pictures of Barbie dolls.

"Janey. Ready for a classic tale of teen suicide teachers will. Not. Stop. Showing us no matter how antsy they get around the goth kids?" she asked.

In response, I passed her a granola bar, and she handed me what looked like a blown-glass apple the size of a golf ball.

"The inside is filled with applesauce, but the exterior cake is orange flavored. Wild, right?" she said.

I didn't really know if it was wild, but like all the pastries Raina had brought me all year in exchange for my more pedestrian Target snacks, it was delicious.

I watched for a minute as Ms. Lydia fought with the DVD machine, putting the captions on Spanish, then French, then Spanish again, when I heard Raina whisper.

"You should do it, you know."

I stared at her, waiting for her to go on, but she had already pulled out her jewelry pliers and was attempting to make a star out of a paper clip. Had Algie told her about the acorn? Or about Gwen? And what did it mean in either case?

"Uh, Raina? I'm going to need you to be a little more specific, please," I said.

"I might have mentioned I'm an empath."

Raina had been mentioning she was an empath since first grade, when she insisted she could sense Tom P.'s general sense of unease before Ranger Joe asked him if he wanted to hold the snake first and Tom started screaming bloody murder.

"Yes . . ." I said, quickly looking up to the front of the room in case I was going to have to deal with an early-morning snake.

"Your inner conflict is giving me a migraine. I'd like to say I'm going to help you out with this because I care, which I do, but seriously, nails on the chalkboard of my soul. Or in my soul. Whatever. Not up to metaphors. Go."

"Away or . . . ?" I asked, wondering if moving to the other side of the room would be enough to give Raina some relief, or if she'd need me to leave the classroom to grab her some Excedrin: Psychic Headache Relief.

"No, *go,* as in, start talking about the question that has been plaguing your soul and is now plaguing my solar plexus."

"And you'll tell me what to do?"

I was only a little embarrassed by how eager I knew I sounded to put the fate of my love life in the adorably manicured hands of Raina. But if life gives you a Technicolor teenage Yoda, are you really going to leave to figure out the force yourself?

"I'm going to listen, actively, and through that act alone, you will be guided toward the answer you've already come to and are now actively trying to silence. Indecision is like a light, unpleasant buzz. Fighting against yourself is what's making me see three Juliets on the screen right now. Go. Talk. Take pity on the emotional intelligence the universe has chosen to bestow on me. And do you have a Vitaminwater? I think I'm a little dehydrated, too."

I dug out a Capri-Sun and watched as Raina punctured the silvery packet in one deft movement, a feat I hadn't pulled off in my entire life — even without other people's emotions crowding in. I took a deep breath, my faith newly restored in her ability to help me. Maybe.

"So, uh, there's this girl—"

"Obviously."

"Right. So we've been talking for a long time, as friends, and I think we could be more than friends. Well, actually, I really hate that phrase and the way that it undervalues platonic friendship. I think we could be friends who also make out. Friends who also make out and don't make out with anyone else." The words poured out of me, everything a half whisper. I tried not to think of the possibility of anyone overhearing me.

"Janey, when the English language is ready to help you, just let it."

"Right. I want to be her girlfriend."

"Cool. So you're not fighting that particular want. What exactly is stopping you from asking her out?"

"You're kidding, right?"

"Yes, right, fear, but let's narrow it down. Fear of rejection, fear of humiliation, fear of a relationship that quickly escalates beyond your capacity for intimacy?"

"Well, a second ago it was just the first two, but—"

"Sorry."

I nodded, and briefly turned my attention to the movie, suddenly grateful that Ms. Lydia had turned it up so loud that nobody noticed the vaguely supernatural therapy session happening in the back row.

I know the play gets a bad rap, but it's not a bad story. I mean, it's a story of incredibly bad problem-solving and decision-making and communication. But I kind of love that scene where they're talking about palmers and palms and you know they just want to quit with the wordplay and make out already, but every era has its required pre–make out flirting rituals. As it played out onscreen, I watched as all three couples in class slowly linked fingers, or in the incredibly bold case of Tim and Cassidy, managed to stealthily get their desks close enough to actually twist their legs together. I was wistful, I was bitter, I was imagining how Gwen and I might slowly and naturally merge while watching two fellow teens write each other sexy sonnets.

The tip of Raina's feathered pink gel pen gently brushing my forehead suddenly pulled me out of my thoughts. "It's fear of loss, too. We have . . . something. We have a text chain and inside jokes and I have a GIF folder I only use with her and if I screw up this, the whole asking her out execution . . . And, I just . . . If she liked me like that, she would have asked, right? That's what bold, confident people do. They don't wait for socially awkward people to do it."

I turned to Raina, who was gingerly nibbling on the granola bar, eyes closed, though I couldn't tell whether she was deep in pain or deep in thought.

"I think what you want me to say is life is risk or take the risk that's worth the reward or whatever. But my power of metaphor creation is back, so we're going to go with this: Pretend you're at the waffle bar," Raina said.

"The waffle bar?"

"You know, like at one of the motels with the flippy waffle iron that has all the syrup and cut up strawberries and stuff?"

"Right."

"Okay, so, you're at the waffle bar, and you see this giant can of whipped cream and you're like, *That is perfect. I'm going to have the most delicious waffle ever, crunchy and light and sweet. This is going to be amazing.* But then, like, someone is hogging the can, and you don't want to ask for it. Or maybe you remember something you read about whipped cream being full of carcinogens or whatever. So you grab your waffle and you sit down and you put some syrup on it, and, like, it's a good waffle, but it's not the waffle you really wanted. So you would have been happier with a yogurt or something rather than this waffle that just reminds you of the waffle you were dreaming of."

"You have some really strong feelings about waffles, Raina."

"You know what I mean."

"Yes. Probably. Just in case . . ."

"Platonic friendships are the best. But that's not what you want with this girl anymore. No matter how much you might enjoy platonically texting, you're always going to be picturing the dream waffle. And that's no way to live. Metaphorically, or otherwise actually. Waffles without whipped cream are pretty much trash."

I put my head on the desk and tried to enjoy what was left of the movie. By the time the bell rang and snapped Ms. Lydia out of whatever she was doing on her phone, Cassidy had brown-gray imprints from the tread of Tim's boot running down her leggings and I had my motivational soundtrack playing in my head. It was the kind of music I blasted before big tests and internship interviews, accompanied by Raina's voice chanting, "Do it, do it, do it," which she had been whispering since (spoiler) Juliet was about to plunge the dagger into her heart. I was going to do it. I was going to ask Gwen out on an actual date. And while official dates weren't really a thing people did at our school, I figured the private-school courtship rules might line up closer to every teen movie I'd ever seen. If nothing else, I had to remove pining from my daily to-do list. When the bell rang, Raina mouthed, "Good luck," before disappearing into the hall. All the color had come back to her face, and she was putting on her giant kitten-ear headphones. I guessed her headache must have finally gone away.

---

## RAINA LAPIERRE, BELOVED HUMAN RAINBOW

Raina was born when the first fairy baby laughed, or possibly when the first Skittles factory opened, or after any number of vaguely fantastical things happened. She walks through life in a cloud of body glitter friends have always been able to tell is just as much for them as it is for her. She's the girl responsible for the sweet note in your locker when you know you need it most, and she always, always has a piece of gum you can have. Wary of being labeled a manic pixie dream girl, a fear she laid out in an op-ed in her middle school newspaper, Raina is never shy when talking about the less than sunny parts of her life. It was those parts that inspired her to create the largest nonprofit dedicated to decorating the offices of other nonprofits and social service buildings.

"There are so many things in the world I can't change. The warmth of this waiting room is not one of them," LaPierre said when asked about her nonprofit's mission. She continues to survive with her many cats, dogs, and various lovers, who could be named, but whom she prefers to refer to only as "a part of our collective."

---

I ducked into the bathroom to make sure I was semi-presentable. I stared into what passes for mirrors at our high school: dented rectangles of semi-reflective metal that are at complete odds with the otherwise fairly modern and impossibly clean facilities. Apparently when they upgraded all the bathrooms in the early 2000s, a student group had rallied to keep the original, severely depressing mirrors to remind girls they're "beautiful no matter what" or something that's totally true when you think about the big picture, but is ultimately not helpful if you're trying to figure out if that spot on your chin is a zit, ketchup, or rust.

Silvery, slightly warped me looked . . . fine, which was a look I had cultivated deliberately since fifth grade, and now, for the first time, was seriously reconsidering. As Algie got closer and closer to becoming an actual Instagram influencer and the goth kids started coordinating their skulls and chains just so, I had always figured that if I kept my style completely tabula rasa, my look would find me. It's possible I had confused the universe with one of those clothing subscription companies.

By the time I got to the caf, my body had begun that unpleasant nervous humming somewhere between forgot-to-eat-breakfast and a high fever, which I felt confident must be a feeling similar to what all pro athletes have right before they are going to absolutely crush it on the court or field or whatever.

I walked confidently toward Algie and Gwen, chanting, "Be. Aggressive. *B-E* aggressive," under my breath, not because I thought you should be aggressive in this kind of a situation, but because I figured if you mixed in some aggression with my doormat tendencies you might get assertiveness — like when you have to mix in acid to a solution that's too base to get a balanced pH. I was going to be so happy to be done with chem, if only to stop thinking in chemical metaphors.

I arrived at our usual table and sat on the bench directly across from Gwen, who was sitting next to Algie.

"So, Gwen, is public school living up to the lack of hype?" I asked, hoping this was a good icebreaker. Algie's lack of facial expressions seemed to imply it was at least neutral.

"Your fries are definitely better than ours. And Algie just introduced me to ketchup plus mayonnaise. It's really too disgusting to even think about eating, but I do like the pink," Gwen said, smiling. God, it was the smiling that threatened to derail this whole asking-out plan.

"I think we need to discuss something important, Janey," Algie said, before I could even start to formulate my pitch. I raised an eyebrow at him, a skill I was very proud of and had worked on for years as a shorthand for *Your cryptic set-up is making me nervous.*

"We need to talk about prom," he clarified, stirring his chocolate pudding like it was a cup of afternoon tea.

"Which prom?" Gwen asked.

"Let's start with the one that serves caviar," Algie said.

"I still hold that that was just black boba they got from the frozen yogurt place across the street," Gwen said, flicking through something on her phone. Actually, less a flick and more of a swipe. Was she on Tinder? Bumble? Some kind of elite dating app where she'd charm potential suitors with the hilarious anecdote of a girl who tried to ask her out and didn't even use primer?

My phone buzzed against my leg. A text from Algie.

> I can tell you're spiraling. Don't worry. I've got this.

"It really doesn't matter if your school was attempting to peddle counterfeit caviar. They thought the student population would want —no, expect—fish eggs, which puts our own public school festivities in a harsh light. What's your theme again, Gwen?" he asked.

"Under the Sea. Pretty standard, I think. Cliché, even."

"If you are getting buzzed under cardboard starfish, absolutely. But this year you'll be celebrating formal wear and chlamydia outbreaks under the . . ."

". . . whale at the Museum of Natural History. But only because our headmaster happens to be related to an administrator there. It's not like museum connections scream 'the one percent.'"

"Janey, would you like to inform Gwendolyn what theme our school deemed appropriately fancy enough for possibly the most formal event our peers might attend in their entire, likely lackluster lives?" Algie asked.

"I don't think there's anything wrong with A Night in Paris," I said, trying to not look like I was trying to catch Gwen's eye, while totally trying to catch Gwen's eye.

"I have nothing against a night that is truly paying tribute to Paris. That is not what's happening. They're serving french fries. Without even the common decency to list them as *pommes frites* on the menu like any other self-respecting institution trying too hard," Algie said with a slight shudder.

"As much as I love your conversation-turned–term paper, Algernon, I think you had a question about prom? Or was that just an excuse to mock my excellent education?" Gwen asked.

"Do you have a date?"

I felt my entire body tense up, terrified to hear her answer.

"I'm going with Jason," Gwen said. I suddenly found myself fascinated by a spot on the table.

"Jason as in the Jason you went to homecoming with sophomore year?" Algie asked.

Gwen had worn a drop-waist lilac gown with her hair half up, half down to homecoming sophomore year. I told myself this knowledge came from my savant-like powers of recall and not my stalker-like tendencies. I also reminded myself not to read too much into the fact that in my memory, Jason's face was just an outline with a question mark, like a placeholder pic before you upload a real photo.

"He's grown a lot in two years," Gwen said, staring down at her phone again, possibly at the apparently incredibly mature Jason.

"You mean his dick?" Algie asked. I thought I might be having a stroke. Or I might have just chosen to have a stroke to keep myself from bearing further witness to this conversation.

"God, all you people ever think of is dick size." Gwen sighed.

"'You people'? Do I have to report a hate crime, Gwen?" Algie asked.

"I meant guys, Algie. The tie that binds, regardless of sexual orientation. No need to call RuPaul."

"Gwendolyn, if I had RuPaul's number, I promise I would have more important things to plan than prom. But back to Jason's growth."

I hoped Jason had a growth. On his nose. Actually, growths all over his face.

"I actually didn't ask for measurements before I agreed to eat fake caviar with him. All I meant was he's a little more up on world events than he was two years ago. Cares about things beyond the confines of the football field. Isn't as prone to yelling, 'Scoooorrre!' when he witnesses PDA," Gwen said. "And, more importantly, he's a Desmond."

"Is that an ancient order of men with oversize —" Algie started before Gwen snaked her arm around his mouth, pressing her forearm into it to shut him up while still holding her cookie aloft, not knocking off a single sprinkle. If she was on *America's Got Talent*, with this move alone she'd totally win.

"A Desmond belongs to one of the five Upstate New York families with roots deep enough, and trust funds big enough, for him to end up on my mom's approved suitor list," Gwen said, degagging Algie and taking another bite of her cookie.

I didn't say anything, lost in thoughts of my family barbecues that involved "the fancy paper plates" because they were thick enough that the barbecue sauce wouldn't leak through. And of how by the time everyone got second helpings, we'd normally run out of the fancy paper plates and had to spend the rest of the night with sticky, smoky streaks across our thighs. Plus, the closest thing I had to a trust fund was a savings account my grandpa opened for me on my thirteenth birthday with thirteen dollars, promising to add an amount that matched my age on my birthday every year. Algie's trust fund countdown clock would end when he turned twenty-one. When I was twenty-one, I'd have $153. Plus interest. I wondered if Sandra Snoot and her mother were the kind of people Gwen's mom would deem fancy enough. I hated that they filled my mind so quickly, sharing space with my actual family—the family that could pick me out of a lineup.

"Yes, my mother's a snob. Your parents are snobs too, they just know you go through guys so quickly that fighting you on your choices would be a full-time job."

"So I'm pretty sure what you're saying is the solution is for you to be more slutty."

"'Be more slutty' is always your solution."

"I'm going to go get something from the vending machine," I said, getting up and walking to the wall of softly glowing machines offering their sugary, salty comfort. Hearing about Gwen's love life, past, present, and future, which didn't seem to have room for even a page on me, let alone a chapter, was not what this lunch period was supposed to be about. It was supposed to be about being bold, and possibly destiny. Standing in front of the machines, I realized I didn't have any cash, and so I had to slink back to the table, empty-handed.

"You should come to ours," Algie finished as I sat back down.

"You want me to crash your prom?" Gwen asked.

"No, I want you to go as Janey's date. Janey, ask Gwen to prom," Algie said, with the exact same tone he'd use if he was asking me to pass the ketchup.

"Algie, what are you doing?" I hissed, horribly aware that no matter how quiet I was, Gwen could hear me. Going to the prom was so much bigger than a date. It was a megadate that came with not just photographic evidence, but photographic evidence that would likely be framed and possibly end up on the local news if you happened to be murdered in any period between prom and your wedding day.

"What? It's the perfect plan. You take Gwen, I take Cecil, we'll make an amazing foursome. And I want credit, Janey, for not making that sexual."

"You don't get any points if you still conjure the image that will be stuck in our brains forever. And since when are you going to ask Cecil to prom? You haven't even hung out alone yet. He might have plans. He might have had a good look at your mentions," I said, hoping that if I talked long enough and fast enough, maybe I'd be able to push through this lunch without having to deal with the Gwen gauntlet Algie just threw down.

"It's possible we went to the movies last Sunday," Algie said, the image of casual.

"What— He— One of you would have told me."

"Usually true, unless—"

"—you saw *Love, Specifically* without me. Asshole."

"I mean, would you have really wanted to be a third wheel to what is soon to be a prom-bound couple?"

"So freakin' arrogant, Algie. You still have to ask him—"

"I asked him, like, two seconds ago. Texted him, got not only an affirmative but a series of GIFs that so perfectly fit the conversation, I suspect he might have a folder labeled 'Romantic Successes,' which I find only slightly sad and mostly incredibly efficient," Algie said, holding up his phone to show me Cecil's rapturous and very Disney-GIF heavy yes to Algie's invitation to prom, which was literally the word *prom* and a question mark. I felt like invitations to the biggest dance in all of high school—dom should fall somewhere in between the kind of promposals that people get arrested for and a single word.

"So, are you going to ask her, or is this going to be a ventriloquism situation?" Algie asked, suddenly hopping up from his seat next to Gwen to come sit next to me, sticking his forearm to my spine as if he were about to open my mouth like those creepy puppets'. I scooched forward on the bench with a jerk, whacking the bottom of my rib cage on the table and sort of unintentionally giving myself the Heimlich maneuver, a piece of granola bar flying out of my mouth and whizzing just past Gwen's head. I died. I was actually dead. There was no point in fighting Algie on this whole prom ask because embarrassment had finally killed me, and they do not allow the dead at prom. Unless you count that musical *Zombie Prom.*

I took a deep, shaky breath, coughed a little on the granola crumbs I'd just unintentionally inhaled, and forced myself to look right at Gwen. I was not going to let Algie ask her out for me. I had some sense of pride — or I would have liked to cultivate some sense of pride at least.

"Algie, I am not asking anyone to prom so casually, or because you suggested it, or with this strong a smell of imitation sausage patties hanging in the air," I said, delivered with all the gravity of a general in a World War II movie telling his men they are about to die, but die with honor.

"Oh wow, is that what that is? I couldn't even think of how to describe the smell to ask about it," Gwen said, with a grimace chased with a grin.

"It is completely singular, and somehow in the caf, ubiquitous. Now — do you want to grab dinner some time? Somewhere that doesn't smell. As a date?"

I was stunned. Algie was stunned. I had pivoted from meatless sausage smell to a date, ignoring the rules of Ms. Manners, any number of teen magazines, the entirety of Reddit's r/relationship thread, and the entire canon of contemporary rom-coms. I wasn't going to just get rejected. I was going to get a peer-recommended trip to the counselor. Just as I was trying to figure out a way to turn this into a fabulous joke, Gwen smiled her beautiful, easy yet deliberate smile.

"I would love to, Janey," Gwen said, just as the bell rang.

Now it was my turn to be in shock, which I know, medically,

keeps you numb from the pain of a shark bite or massive car crash. But it was now keeping my body from exploding with joy.

"I'll text you . . . things," I called after her as she followed Algie to the trash incinerator. As she dumped her tray in, Algie turned toward me and gave me a series of looks I almost wished I couldn't translate but totally could — *Good job, I'm proud of you, you are so in over your head.*

I grinned back, a very translatable look.

I watched them both walk out of the cafeteria, feeling a buzz against my leg what seemed like half a second later. I knew it was a text from Algie, but I let it vibrate as I walked down the hall to Spanish. Before I got a list of advice, before I considered the perfect spot to bring her, before I thought about possible outfits, I was going to bask in this moment, in the glorious, momentarily uncomplicated knowledge that I had a date with Gwendolyn Fairfax. And possibly more importantly, I hadn't scared her off by accidentally spitting my snack at her hair. It made me believe that maybe there was hope for us yet.

# CHAPTER FOUR

**The suspense is terrible. I hope it will last.**

—OSCAR WILDE, *THE IMPORTANCE OF BEING EARNEST*

After a way-too-long subway ride home (Algie said he had to stay late for drama club), I practically limped up the stairs to my room, physically and mentally exhausted, the high of Gwen's yes morphing into a low-humming anxiety. When I got upstairs, I tossed my phone on the bed without looking, a years-old reflex that combined the certain forbidden air of chucking a more than five-hundred-dollar life-sustaining implement made out of glass clear across the room with the fluffy safety net of a hoarder's nest of pillows, stuffed animals, and printed fleece blankets. What can I say? I like to be cozy. I had, up until this point, never thought my Apple™ toss would cause any undue harm or bloodshed. But I had also never anticipated finding Gwen on my bed. Or Gwen's face ending up in the dead center of the trajectory of my phone's glorious arch.

"Well, I think my glasses took most of that," Gwen said, with the kind of calm I thought you could only achieve through becoming a Buddhist monk or possibly smoking those cigarettes from the '50s without the filters.

"Oh my god, I am so sorry. I never really look before I throw it.

You're okay?" I asked, totally breathless because I had just assaulted her and because I was realizing Gwen was on my bed. If I'd had to write a list of the top ten places I would have liked Gwen to be, all ten would have been my bed.

"I mean, even if you had seen me, you would have been well within your rights to throw your phone at me. I'm a home invader. You were just defending yourself," Gwen said with a smirk, examining a crack my phone had left in the right lens of her sunglasses, which I assumed she had been wearing because people with a certain level of mysterious poise are not governed by the laws of light and dark, night and day, inside and outside.

"Algie told me the shortcut," Gwen said, her gaze moving off the glasses and onto me. The "shortcut" was a fairly solid oak outside my room with more than enough branches and knots for any reasonably athletic child to climb. But my best friend, who was, despite his best efforts, passably athletic but thoroughly unreasonable, had inserted climbing-wall grabbing stones along the tree trunk all the way to the top when we were eight. At the time it had seemed like a ridiculous display of laziness. But after the first few times I found Algie in my bed after he had snuck a bottle of wine or two from his parents' liquor cabinet, I was kind of glad he had some assistance.

"I know Algie loves to make an entrance, but you could have used the door," I said.

"Oh, I know, but . . . parents. They just ask so many questions, you know?" Gwen said, not flopping, but gracefully reclining on what I realized, in mild horror, was a particularly large clump of vintage Pound Puppies I had inherited from a twice-removed cousin.

"My parents aren't that inquisitive," I lied, knowing full well that if my mother knew I had a girl in my room, she would demand the door be kept open, the music turned down, and the girl's full name texted to her ASAP so she could begin googling.

"Must be nice. My mother is now on her third private investigator. This year," Gwen said.

"That— That is impressive. Who's she trying to find?" I asked.

"Oh, Mom knows where everyone is. She's trying to find out what everyone is doing. Last week it was my sister's new boyfriend. Wall Street, but no trust fund. And you know what they say—*they* being the women at my mother's Junior League meeting—about men without trust funds," she said.

"That you can't trust them?" I guessed, eager to play rich-kid Mad Libs if it would prove to Gwen that I'd gotten closer to a country club than watching the end of *Dirty Dancing*.

"Probably. I don't know. I tune them out most of the time," she said, picking up my Pound Puppy Michael, which in her hands looked more like a hopeful rescue from the pound than an overly cherished stuffed animal, and stared into his round, painted-on eyes.

"I like your stuffed animal collection. Mother wouldn't even get us Barbies. She said they're tacky. Charlotte and I have a shelf each of porcelain dolls. You can't cuddle with porcelain dolls. Charlotte tried. She rolled over in her sleep, shattered its face, and ended up with a shard of Little Bo-Peep's cheek lodged in her back," Gwen said with more nonchalance than I could imagine ever having about that situation.

"Oh my god. Was she okay?" I asked.

"It left a pretty nasty-looking two-inch scar. Our mother makes her use concealer when she wears backless dresses. You'd think she would consider it a badge of honor. There are few things as intensely bougie as getting your only childhood scar from an honest-to-god porcelain doll," she said, smiling, which made me smile, then seemed to pull me toward her until I was sitting next to Gwen on my bed, our knees only the width of a Pound Puppy's head apart.

"So with the whole throwing things at you, and then that story, I haven't really gotten a chance to ask. Why are you here? Not that I don't want you here. You're totally welcome to climb my tree anytime," I said quickly, realizing too late that "climb my tree" sounded vaguely like some kind of daring sex act.

"Right. You distracted me from the task at hand," she said.

The idea I could possibly distract Gwen made me dizzy. Which was probably why I dared put my hand on her knee. To steady myself. I used to mock purposely ripped jeans, but I found myself thanking whatever Levi's designer was responsible for the sudden contact between my hand and Gwen's partially bare leg.

"We're kidnapping you to drag you to a loft party. Which I know sounds a little overdone. But I've received multiple texts from my most discerning classmates, who have assured me it strikes just the right balance between *Gossip Girl* and *Gone Girl*. Should I grab your purse?"

"We?" I had barely gotten out the question when Algie's head popped up in my window like some kind of life-size jack-in-the-box.

"The royal *we*," he clarified as he slithered in through the window, only to lean back out it again to offer a hand to . . . a very shaken and yet radiantly happy Cecil.

"So I guess drama practice . . ." I started.

". . . was a ruse to get Cecil without your judgy looks. Or, I guess, before your judgy looks. Don't look at me like that. The poor boy has never been to a loft party. How will he ever become a New Yorker without watching our city's finest youth use Brooklyn's most twee coke spoons?"

I watched Cecil's eyes go dinner-plate big as he tried to work out exactly how much cocaine these people were ingesting if they had to use a spoon.

"Cecil, he's joking. You're joking, right?" I asked, suddenly remembering that people Gwen went to school with actually could have a more expensive vice than hard cider.

"There was one guy, Guy?"

"Right, right, Guy the guy, he got shipped to rehab sophomore year, I think, but the Quads have a pretty strict 'If you can't have a good time with vodka, we don't want you at our party anyway' vibe, so —" Gwen said, as she began to explore the cluster of bags hanging on a hook off the back of my door, which weren't really purses so much as tote bags I got for free at events of varying degrees of nerdiness.

Gwen grabbed the handles of the largest tote — one with a white, screen-printed acronym I had absolutely no recollection of — and put it on the bed.

"It's smart to go with totes. You don't have to carry any of your stuff in your hands, and it's no big deal if you spill a drink on it.

Practical," Gwen said. I could feel my heart sink a little. *Practical* is not sexy. *Practical* is not interesting. The only thing worse than being described as *practical* is *sensible*, because that means that in addition to being boring, you might try to drag your friends down to your own mundane level.

"So, um, the loft party. I'm going to have to give my parents the details. I know there won't be supervision," Cecil said in a whisper, staring not at his own shoes, but at Algie's purple high-tops, as if not even in his moment of mortification could he bear to take his eyes off him.

"Oh no, Jack and Jill will make an appearance. Real names, swear to god, and real parents, if only legally. They believe teenagers should drink in the home, and they also don't really like their kids much, so they try to limit their stays during parties to appearances and selfie opportunities. But your parents can call them for assurance that the party will be chaperoned," Gwen said.

"So they're just going to lie?" I asked, trying not to sound totally scandalized.

"No, they have a nanny cam–equipped robot butler, so if there's any murder, intentional or unintentional, it'll be hard to pin on anyone but the murderer," Gwen said, because apparently Algie was right —her life was just a series of almost–20/20 episodes.

"It's themed, by the way," Gwen added, as she got up and went toward the window, my tote bag thrown over her shoulder. "You're going to want to wear your best underwear."

I caught Cecil's eyes, which morphed from dinner plates to those big platters my dad saves for the Thanksgiving turkey.

I swallowed. I would be brave. Brave for Cecil, who looked slightly faint. Brave in the afterglow of touching Gwen's knee. Brave because I was pretty sure brave people had more exciting lives, and I was starting to realize that was an adjective I wanted attached to mine.

"I love theme parties," I said, smiling.

---

After some party prep (embraced by Cecil and Algie, totally unnecessary for Gwen, and forced for me) we were on the downtown 6 train rocketing toward a fancy apartment in a fancy neighborhood. I still was not at all sure I would be shedding my not-so-fancy jeans and T-shirt to reveal my least holey pair of underwear and one bra without stains or the underwire poking out. I apparently lived in a near constant threat of dying by impalement on my own lingerie.

"So, um, how do you know . . . actually, I don't think you told me the name of Jack and Jill's kid," I asked Gwen, trying to subtly clench and unclench my abs in an attempt to make my stomach more presentable. She and Algie sat across from Cecil and me in the two corner double seaters.

"Four kids, actually. The Quads. Four aspiring models with identical smiles, biceps, and loud opinions on things they have no actual knowledge of. I don't think I can pin down where our paths first crossed, but I'm going to go ahead and guess . . . my second pre-K?"

"The one your mom pulled you out of when she found out they didn't offer Mandarin?" Algie asked, suddenly standing up to hang off the subway pole *Singing in the Rain*–style.

"No, that was the first one. I left Young Minds United after a teacher's aide dared to give us Lunchables."

"No! Not with processed cheese," Algie yelped in mock horror.

"So processed. My poor delicate palate was so confused. I even ate the little red stick you use to spread the cheese on the crackers."

"Guys, sorry to break up this really specific childhood memory, but I think we're here," I said, grabbing the dangling strap of Cecil's backpack to lead him off the train, an old-school habit that at times seemed overly childish, but was also really practical.

We stayed stitched together up the steps, following Algie and Gwen, breaking apart only when we were standing in front of the doorman to explain we were guests of Jack, Jill, and their children, Dave, Doug, Damon, and Don.

The elevator didn't stop at a single floor separating the lobby from the penthouse — I guess when you live in a spectacularly fancy apartment, you don't really feel like leaving that much.

As it climbed, Algie dug a ChapStick out of Gwen's purse, then, after putting some on while keeping shameless eye contact with Cecil, he yelled, "Catch," and tossed it at Gwen. Without looking up, she caught it in one hand, and I felt my knees go a little weak. Apparently, I find good hand-eye coordination incredibly sexy.

In front of the Quad's door, Gwen rang the doorbell and we stood in only slightly awkward silence. I knew neither Algie nor Cecil could stand the quiet for more than a minute or two, and I started humming "The Final Countdown" to myself waiting to see who would crack first.

"My boxers have cats on them," Cecil said, too loudly, too

excitedly, too everything. I could barely look at Algie. He was never going to let that awkwardness go—

"You are adorable," he said smiling in Cecil's direction.

Before they could say anything else, the door swung open and the human equivalent of a pack of four purebred golden retrievers was staring back at us.

"We thought you might be food," Quad 1 said.

"Well, technically—" said another, before being cut off by Quad 3.

"I said no cannibalism talk at this party."

"You did not."

"Well, it was implied."

"Guys, shut up, you're freaking out Gwen's friends."

"Jesus, that one does look freaked. Why is she so pale?"

"Just because your girlfriend takes a freakin' bath in that tanning crap—"

"Lay off Jessica. I told you, she just gets a natural tan really quickly—"

"She stained Lucy, Don. We had a brown-streaked Samoyed for weeks."

"Quads!" Gwen didn't quite shout, more commanded, snapping the puppy boys' attention to her in an instant. She was so powerful. I sent her a silent thank-you, unable to keep track of which Quad was talking when.

"Your four-man show is almost ready. Seriously, keep workshopping it. But if you could chill for a second. Also, Janey isn't pale; she just has gorgeous porcelain skin that, yes, certain tanning habits of our peers have made less common."

I waved, which felt bizarre even as I was doing it, but there was no way I was going to be forming words so soon after Gwen used *gorgeous* to describe me. I mean, yes, technically she said my skin was gorgeous, but the skin is the largest organ, so if my skin was gorgeous, that must mean a solid percentage of me was gorgeous too, right?

"She looks familiar," said a Quad.

Before one of his brothers could chime in, a very tan, very tall girl in a purple silky bra and panty set breezed by the door, stopping to consider us for a moment before saying without any real meanness or, really, interest, "She's Bag Baby Babe," and walked on.

We were then ushered into the front room, where we were instantly confronted with a living Victoria's Secret ad. Except absolutely no one was in need of airbrushing. What's good about clothes, I realized, is that in addition to keeping you warm and sometimes informing strangers of your fandoms, they leave a certain amount of mystery about exactly how hot people who aren't you are. I mean, yes, when you see someone in a skintight T-shirt and skinny jeans that you're not one hundred percent sure aren't tattooed onto their perfect legs, you know they are, in and out of clothes, objectively hot. But there's also the possibility those clothes are masking some errant patch of cellulite, or a third nipple poking out of their sternum, or any other kind of mark that wouldn't really dim their attractiveness but let all of us more average individuals have a moment of peace.

There would be no peace at this party. Just a complete lack of body fat coupled with what I assumed was the kind of skincare regimen I could never seem to master no matter how many trips I took to Sephora. I had almost, almost psyched myself up to slip out of my jeans (and when I say *slip*, I really mean *manically wiggle*) when a girl passed with what I thought was a butterfly tattoo on her upper thigh, only to realize, suddenly, that it was actually a birthmark. I could not be naked with people who even have perfect birthmarks.

"I think I'm going to change in the bathroom," I whispered to Algie, who had already disrobed and was talking to Cecil, who had also taken off his jeans to reveal not just cat, but Grumpy Cat, boxers, which were somehow both at odds with and oddly complemented by his cat socks.

Algie didn't even glance in my direction, and I thought for a second he might be ignoring me completely until he yelled, "Gwen, Janey wants to see the library."

I was so distracted by the stress of becoming a human version of those *Highlights* magazine "Can you spot the one thing that doesn't fit in this scene" puzzles, I hadn't even noticed Gwen had ended up on the other side of the room. I could see the top of her head moving through the gaggle of beautiful people, just a little above them because sometimes life is perfectly metaphorical like that. Then suddenly she was right in front of me, in a lacy white bralette and black boy shorts that didn't match or even vaguely coordinate but somehow worked perfectly for her.

"Janey, you seem a little overdressed," she smiled.

And before I could come up with a witty retort, pretty much before my brain could even form the directive "Need witty retort,"

Gwen was unzipping my hoodie. I decided to let it fall to the ground, partly because I had a vague sense that letting clothes simply fall off you was inherently hot, and partly because my arms had gone completely numb.

"You think you can handle your jeans yourself?" she asked with a smile, and I nodded because I'd been taking off my own jeans for at least a decade. I figured muscle memory like that can't disappear, even in the face of some slight lust-related nerve damage. So I unzipped, and I wiggled, and then I was less than a foot away from Gwendolyn Fairfax, neither of us able to go to a McDonald's and get service.

"I like your outfit," Gwen said. She might've been whispering, but it was hard to tell the actual volume since the entire party seemed to be drowned out by the sound of my own heartbeat pounding in my ears.

"Yours too," I eeked out, maintaining eye contact because that's what the confidence-building book I had read last semester suggested . . . and because I was suddenly terrified that if I let it break, I might try to kiss her. I'd spent enough time with Algie to know that flirting when performed by the truly confident is not an invitation to actually make out. I didn't think I could handle rejection in front of fifty strangers who had never actually experienced bloating.

"So, I'm guessing Algie was speaking on your behalf again when he demanded I show you the library, but it is pretty amazing, if you want to check it out," Gwen said. Before I could nod, she began guiding me though the kitchen, past Algie showing Cecil something on his phone, all the way to the back of the apartment.

I let her open the door, and then walked into the kind of home library I hadn't even been sure existed outside of murder mystery novels and episodes of *Law & Order* when the murderer is loaded — i.e., complete floor-to-ceiling bookshelves. I was taking it all in when I realized all the books were the same color, like the exact same shade, and size and shape. I watched as Gwen brushed a row with her finger, selected a title, pulled it off the shelf, and handed it to me.

It was heavy, but not a solid heavy like I'd expected. It kind of . . . sloshed?

Gwen took it back and opened it, revealing a hollow spot housing a silver flask.

"Hollow? Yes. Full of booze? Not entirely. Some have candy and I believe we found one full of fortune cookie slips at another party. Don swears one has their birth certificates all folded up, but I don't really believe that."

"Rich people, man. They should really make a TV show about you guys."

"They have. Repeatedly, actually."

Then we were both laughing, and I noticed how my laugh was almost the exact same pitch as hers, or maybe the same tone. Either way, it was some measure of sound that disappeared into hers almost seamlessly.

"You know, I'm really looking forward to our date, Janey," she said, suddenly looking at me intently.

"You are?" I asked, cursing myself for demanding validation, for being needy. But I did need, so often, and maybe not wearing that on my sleeve meant not being honest. Of course, at the moment, I didn't have any sleeves, so —

Normally getting lost in my head meant I'd miss a question the teacher just asked, or nearly walk into traffic before Algie pulled me back. But tonight, it meant I didn't realize Gwen was going to kiss me until she was actually kissing me. It was the nicest surprise I'd ever gotten.

Being kissed by the girl you've been dreaming about since middle school is actually a lot like passing out. Everything gets a little dimmer, and for a few seconds, you're not sure where you are or who you are, just that things are hazy and unfocused. The feeling was absolutely gorgeous, as Gwen would probably say. That seemed like the only worthwhile word for it—and for Gwen. What a gorgeous moment. But then she stopped, her face hovering over mine, and my mind was suddenly very, very awake. Should I say something? Should I thank her? Years of living in the world told me that wasn't something I should do, but it felt weird not to express gratitude when I'd never been so thankful for anything in my entire life.

Before I could embarrass myself further, her lips brushed gently against my neck, and my mind went deliciously blank. Or really, my brain became wonderfully focused, nothing but *Gwen Gwen Gwen* playing on repeat. I felt like I should do something with my hands. I wanted to do a lot with my hands. I wanted to test out the limits of their dexterity in ways I never had before. And yet my arms remained glued to my sides, meaning Gwen was actually making out with someone suffering from locked-in syndrome.

"Are you . . . Is this okay?" she whispered by my ear, and I knew this was it, this was when I would pull her closer, when I'd run a finger down her spine like a really sexy scoliosis test, when I'd go from a passive participant in the greatest moment of my life to an active player!

"Yup" was all I said. Because I am a wuss. I expected Gwen to jump back in disgust at my cowardice, or at least in boredom. But instead, I heard her giggle. I had never heard Gwen, the most glamourous girl I knew, giggle. It sounded fantastic.

"You're not usually a woman of few words," she said, before her face was over mine again, so painfully beautiful with this new expression, not amused, not pleased, just . . . happy.

Then she was kissing me again, and I couldn't even beat myself up for my still-immobile arms. Because they weren't frozen in fear anymore. Instead, I had melted and was now a puddle of joyous Janey goo. I made Gwen happy.

And then we were interrupted by a thud against the door. Then another. Then yelling. Then smashing. It was possible some of the build-up noises had happened while Gwen was running her tongue down the side of my neck, but I just kind of figured auditory hallucinations might be a side effect of your mind being completely blown. What really got us untangled was a very interesting yell, so loud it was crystal clear even through the door.

"Are you saying you wouldn't give me a kidney? Right now, in this moment, that's what you're saying to me?"

I looked at Gwen, who looked back at me for a second before the door burst open and Algie and Cecil were there. Algie's arm was casually slung around Cecil's waist, which was still covered by his T-shirt.

"Kristy is drunk. It's time for the live entertainment portion of the party," Algie said. Gwen grabbed my hand as we followed them into the living room area.

"Algie, aren't, like, most people drunk this far into a party? I saw the liquor cabinet coming in. I don't think most actual bars stock that much alcohol" I heard Cecil say. He kept tilting his head toward Algie's shoulder, then snapping it back, afraid to commit to such a couple-y pose. So not only was Algie going break his heart, but he was also going to give Cecil lifelong neck pain.

"They can get a little cautionary tale–esque, but—" Algie started, before Gwen cut him off.

"—there aren't a lot of people who really get sloppy, except for Kristy," Gwen finished, and flicked her hand toward a girl I assumed was Kristy standing on top of a coffee table, pointing a very realistic-looking sword at one of the Quads.

"Kristy, you don't need a kidney," he said, kind of dismissively, I thought, for someone with a large sharp thing pointed at his exposed torso.

"That is not the *point!*" she screeched, suddenly jamming the tip of the sword into the table, where it stuck, like the sword in the stone.

"Kristy. Sweetie. I've got Goldfish. Pizza Goldfish. You want some Goldfish?" a girl in a green satin slip asked, waving a bag of snacks in the direction of her face.

"I don't want Goldfish. I want loyalty!" she said, seemingly on the verge of tears.

"I'll give you a kidney, Kristy, okay? I'll totally do it, like, just sign me up," said the Quad, fist bumping his brother, I guess for being such a caring and sensitive boyfriend.

"You — you promise? I just need to know where we are, you know?" Kristy asked as she bent over and ripped the sword from the mahogany in a pretty impressive show of strength and coordination for someone so far down the tequila hole.

"Oh my god, should we call someone?" Cecil asked, echoing what I had just been wondering silently.

"You want to be the one to explain this to the 911 operator?" Algie asked. "It'll be fine. This isn't even the biggest weapon Kristy's pointed at Damon."

I was about to ask what, exactly, the biggest weapon was when apparently Damon asked, "Babe, you gonna put the sword down?"

"I need. To know. You know, beauty — it's only as deep as you make it. You know? I need to know," she sniffed, as she raised the sword and brought it down, horrifyingly fast, on the top of her side ponytail, shearing it. It seemed like the entire party froze, staring at the fallen pony lying at Kristy's feet. Her eyes were huge, and even though I didn't think she really understood what she had just done, I also thought that there's got to be some kind of primal fear triggered when you can feel a large quantity of your own hair tickling your toes.

"Damon, am I bald now?" she asked in a whisper.

"Not quite, babe. But you're still totally hot," he answered.

Squealing, Kristy let herself kind of fall into Damon's arms.

"That's actually really sweet," Cecil said, almost at the exact same time Gwen said, "Disaster," and Algie said, "The hottest of all hot messes."

I could feel their eyes on me, like they were waiting for me to weigh in on the tableau, something I didn't think I'd feel comfortable doing even if I wasn't riding the high from Gwen's lips on my neck. Still, I felt like I had to say something.

"It's all three, guys. It's totally all three."

# CHAPTER FIVE

**The good ended happily, and the bad unhappily. That is what Fiction means.**

−OSCAR WILDE, *THE IMPORTANCE OF BEING EARNEST*

I really had thought that going on a date with Gwen post-hookup would take some of the pressure off. I mean, while Algie making out with someone might mean little beyond him being in a WiFi dead zone and needing a little entertainment, I was pretty sure Gwen kissing me (and kissing me and kissing me) meant this was definitely not a pity date and she was at least attracted to me. But as completely Cirque du Soleil–level mesmerizing as the evening had been, I had to admit we hadn't done an enormous amount of talking. This opened up the horrifying possibility that I could turn her off with my personality, which was a possibility I was so much less ready to bear than the thought she was repulsed by, say, my slightly asymmetrically aligned eyebrows.

I unfortunately made the mistake of sharing my nerves with Mom, Dad, and Cecil, who all had their well-meaning contributions that just ratcheted my stress levels up even more. My phone buzzed all day with a mix of sports stats from my dad ("They're great filler for when the conversation stalls!"), affirmations from my mom that were supposed to be empowering, but seemed to anticipate the date going poorly ("'No one can make you feel inferior without your consent' — Eleanor Roosevelt/*The Princess Diaries*") and GIFs of various baby animals smiling from Cecil. The only one not making my phone ding every two seconds was Algie, who unloaded all his sage advice as he helped me get ready. Or, as he put it, helped me find the ready I didn't even know I had within me (he'll never let me forget the month I kind of got sucked into my mom's self-help books).

"What look are you going for — classic? Retro? Bold? Understated? I need keywords," Algie said as he bent over my second dresser drawer, which was full of mostly free T-shirts from charity walks and summer camp. I didn't know what fashion category they fit into. Grunge, maybe?

"I'm dressed, Algie. This is what I'm wearing. You're here for moral support, not outfit support," I said, sweeping my arm, Vanna White–style, across my body to show off the light blue sundress with purple piping around the edges. I had no strong feelings about the color or style, but when I put it on in the dressing room at T.J.'s, there were very few parts of my body I wanted to suck in or push out, and that had always been my fashion goal.

"First of all, I'm here for all the support. I am here to offer you guidance in all facets of your life. Lean on me when you're not et cetera, et cetera. Second — holy — don't move. There's a spider on your shoulder, and I think I can see its teeth."

I suddenly became aware of a weight on my shoulder, and my vision blackened around the edges. Sick surges of adrenaline coursed hot and cold through my limbs. I felt like I was going to pass out, but

I was also aware that if I did pass out, I'd end up on the floor, which might anger the spider, or fling it onto my face, or both.

"Get it, get it, get it," I whispered, barely breathing so I wouldn't disturb it. I watched as Algie tiptoed until we were only a few inches apart, then put his hands on either side of my face.

"Janey, there is no spider. But I wanted you to know, whatever happens tonight, it won't be as scary as this moment," Algie said, grabbing me in a half hug, half catch as all the fear that had been holding me upright disappeared.

"I hate you," I whispered in his ear, my suddenly very heavy head resting on his shoulder.

"You love me," he replied, patting me on the head and then gently depositing me onto my bed.

"It's purely Stockholm syndrome," I muttered as I raked my fingers through my hair, trying to puff it up a little.

"So, where are you guys going?" Algie asked.

"That burger place that serves the scary-big milkshakes with the whole pieces of cake speared on the straw," I answered, looking at myself in the mirror. I wasn't sure if I needed eyeliner. I was even less sure whether I could hold my hand steady enough to try to put on eyeliner.

"That's a lot of sugar for a first date. You didn't just want to go to Petey's or something? Hold on to the comforting familiarity of the Parmesan shakers full of salt and the saltshakers full of something not even a forensic expert could identify?" Algie asked.

"No, I wanted to go somewhere different. Exciting."

Somewhere that I might have noticed Gwen had liked on Instagram a few months ago.

"Janey. Janey. Jane Worthing, stop," Algie said. I didn't know what he was talking about until he took the flat iron out of my hand, revealing a not completely burnt, but almost bizarrely flat piece of my own hair. It's possible Algie was there for more than just moral support.

Algie sat on the floor, back against my bed, and pulled me down from the bed to follow him.

"You're freaking out," he said, rhetorically.

"Possibly."

"Stop."

"Cool. Got it. Will immediately stop the conscious decision I was making to be sweaty and nauseous and questioning my fundamental state of being. Thanks for the advice."

"Everything is going to be fine."

"Everything?"

"Everything involved in your date is going to be fine. I believe in you."

I snorted. Algie scooted until he was across from me, knees touching knees, looking dead serious.

"Janey, you are brilliant and talented and my cousin would be lucky to share a milkshake that will probably kill you both, but death by sugar and love sounds like a pretty good way to die in New York City."

I wanted desperately to believe Algie. But I didn't really have any proof I was brilliant or talented. I had experimented with almost every kind of art and had nothing but a collection of very sad pinch pots to show for it. I couldn't sing. I couldn't play any instruments or sports. I was okay at school, and less than okay at interpersonal skills. I was trying to think of a way to explain my painful mediocrity without sounding too whiny when Algie ducked past me and pulled out my shoebox of notebooks from under my bed. I rolled by eyes.

"The undead obits don't prove anything, Algie. They prove that I'm morbid. They prove that I inherited this specific form of morbidness from my mom."

Just saying *inherit* made the back of my throat sting and burn like I was getting a cold. I got angry sometimes that so many words could still hurt me, even when I thought I'd convinced myself that they couldn't.

"The undead obits are funny and smart and nice in a way that isn't corny, which is a lost art. You think about people, Janey. You write about every single one of these people like they matter, and you're a good writer. And I don't know how you're doing it, but you've managed to smear your waterproof mascara. Luckily, Gwen isn't the kind of person who would write you off for something so superficial."

"It's weird when you get sincere, Algie."

"You know I'd never let anyone say anything bad about you. And that includes you. With the exception of the internet, you are the number one bully I've had to protect you from. And now you have the opening for your first therapy session."

"You don't think there might be some other detail of my life that might go first?" I asked.

"I don't know. Is there?" Algie asked, staring into my soul.

76

I bit my lip. I scratched an itch on my arm that wasn't there. I tried to think of other ways to cause tiny flash points of pain that might distract me from the question Algie wasn't quite asking.

"Do you think Sandra Snoot is real? And really my cousin?" I asked.

"What do you mean? You think I gave fake DNA results?"

"No, but like, what if some of the Bag Baby Babe jerks—"

"Janey, after you left that one night, I did a little research. Just in case. Not that I was going to follow up without you or anything. I dug around and found her Insta, and a page for the place where she works . . . she's real. And don't freak out, or freak out more, but . . . you kind of look like her. Like, not twinning level or anything but there's . . . you know, a family resemblance."

I closed my eyes. A family resemblance. It was actually something I had heard before. My parents and I are three extremely pale white people with various shades of brown hair. Strangers see what they want to see. Waitresses and old people waiting for the bus have felt compelled to tell me I look just like my mother, or my father, or both. We never correct them. Not once had one of us said, "Actually, she's adopted, so not only are you wrong, you're bringing up some stuff that maybe we don't want to deal with while we're trying to enjoy our burgers." But I've never seen it. Maybe I kind of want to see it. I want it to not matter to me so badly. But it does.

"I don't know what to do with it, Algie. With her. With this information. You pick."

"I can't."

"You can. You love to pick."

"I know. But you need to pick this one."

I opened my eyes. Algie smiled at me, the way you'd smile at someone about to take the SATs — a mixture of pity and encouragement.

"Can I decide after my date?" I asked.

"I think that's the best plan," he said.

After a little evening out with my flat iron, I said goodbye to Algie and my parents. I wanted to take the subway alone. Not to be alone with my thoughts, which I didn't want to be with even at an overcrowded party, but to be alone with Sinéad O'Connor. I know it's probably bad luck to listen to a breakup song on the way to a first date. But nothing calms me down like the rhythm of the 7 train and "Nothing Compares to U" blasting out of my earbuds.

Seven stops and two blocks later I was in the booth, waiting for Gwen, willing myself not to pick up my phone again, because I felt like that would make it seem like I wasn't living in the moment. On the other hand, it felt really weird just to be staring out into space, with nothing to do with my hands. I kind of wished I was at Petey's. They gave you a piece of pizza dough to play with while you waited.

"You are really staring that picture of a burger down."

I jumped and then watched as Gwen slid into the booth across from me. Her hair was down, loose around her shoulders, which were completely bare in an off-the-shoulder purple top.

"I've always wanted to try this place," she said, grabbing a menu. I almost blurted, "I know," which would have been super creepy, but I managed to keep my mouth shut. If I could make it through the entire dinner without ever opening my mouth, that would be good. Other problems might come up, but nothing that could really rival the damage I could do by talking.

"So I don't know if this is rude, but I've kind of always wanted to ask you . . . what's it like to be famous?" she asked, wrapping her straw wrapper around her finger.

"I'm not famous," I said, too quickly maybe. I wasn't being defensive, really. It was just the truth.

"You have a Wikipedia page," she said.

"You looked me up?"

"Of course."

*Of course* in this situation could mean so many things — that it was normal for Gwen to google everyone even tangentially in her life or that you'd always research a meme you've met IRL. Her googling didn't necessarily mean that it was obvious Gwen had been thinking about me and wanted more information about me, which would lead to even more thinking about me. I considered the question again.

"Well, the Wikipedia page is hardly anything. Probably half of those links are broken, and it's all speculation. Mostly, I'm lucky. No one recognizes me. I can't even imagine what it must be like for people who went viral as adults, who are just, like, at the pharmacy or something, having the kind of day when you'd give anything for the power of invisibility, and some stranger taps them on the shoulder and is like, 'No way, Meatloaf Man!'" I shuddered at the mere thought of surprise social interaction.

"Algie told me about the . . ." I froze. Algie had told her about the acorn? I was going to kill him. Seriously, he was going to get to experience a true crime firsthand.

"I don't even know if it's real. I mean, I guess she's probably real, but what does it matter if I have a cousin and an aunt? Plenty of people have no relationship with their extended family, and I already have an extended family, and when you keep extending things, they have a tendency to snap—"

"Janey? I have no idea what you're talking about. I was going to say Algie told me about the creeps who made the whole Bag Baby Babe thing," Gwen said, unmistakable pity in her expression, though it was hard to tell exactly why she felt bad for me — because of the sexual harassment, or because I had just brought up a painful family secret on a first date, or a little bit of both. I dug my nails into my thigh, trying to steady myself and not throw up, to laugh everything off despite the knowledge that the only thing stopping me from finding answers about where I came was me and, weirdly, a comment that would be burned in my brain forever no matter how many times I tried to forget it: "Whoever left you never would have if they knew you'd grow up to have tits like that." It wasn't the most graphic Bag Baby Babe comment by a long shot. I spent more time looking up words on Urban Dictionary that week than I had in all of middle school combined. It was just the idea that there could be someone out there who didn't know me but knew enough to remind me I had been abandoned while objectifying me. Like some kind of horrific chimera of middle school bully and pick-up artist

I realized, with horror, I had been silent for too long. The moment had crossed over from awkward into super awkward territory. Gwen, in a gesture of infinite kindness and poise, was looking at the menu. She slid it over to me when she saw me look up, pointing to a milkshake topped with two ice cream sandwiches and a plume of cotton candy sprinkled with Skittles. It looked disgusting. It was a masterpiece.

"Want to share?" she asked. I nodded. It was cliché, but the idea of sharing a milkshake with Gwen seemed, in that moment, wonderfully romantic. I fought to keep my swoon strictly internal.

"So, that, um, ramble, about the cousin . . ." I started after we'd given the waitress our order.

"You don't have to explain. It seemed like maybe something you would be pissed about if Algie had told me," she said.

"Not you, specifically! I mean, it's not something I want to talk about, or can talk about, because I'm still in the not-so-good-at-thinking-about-it mode, and I normally like to perfect the thinking portion, before moving on . . . to . . . the talking portion," I said.

"I get that," Gwen said, which was kind of miraculous, because I didn't really get what I had just said. What did Dad always say, Your true love is someone who understands you better than you understand yourself? I had always thought that made the bar for my soulmate a little low because there were times I barely understood myself at all.

"But I do want to explain, er, clarify—" I took a deep breath. "Algie sent my DNA in to one of those family-tree companies, and I got a familial match, and now I have a biological cousin and aunt, but it kind of seems like a dead end because my aunt was adopted, so I'm not sure they can help me find my bio parents, not that I need to, so really, what's the point, except maybe meeting them could be the point? So, yeah." I somehow got out all the pertinent info in one single stream of pure word vomit. I sat and waited for Gwen to say something. Anything.

"There was a week where I thought my dad wasn't my dad," Gwen said.

That was . . . not what I was expecting. She didn't look down, even for a second, which I didn't think I'd ever get used to. I couldn't even keep direct eye contact with Algie. "What are you hiding, Worthing?" he'd joke with me sometimes when I dropped my gaze for the hundredth time. I'd started to wonder how much of a joke it actually was.

"What do you mean?" I asked.

"My cousin — not Algie, Rick — was being a jerk. Telling me he had heard his mom and my mom talking, and my mom admitted she had had an affair and my biological father was a drifter. Really, that should have tipped me off, because we don't really get a lot of drifters in our neighborhood, mostly because we don't live in a novel set in the '20s, but, you know, I was eleven, I didn't know anything. And I look nothing like my father. Like, you know how babies are supposed to look like their dads, so their caveman senses will make them want to provide bottles and board books? My dad must have really had to push past that evolutionary gap. Anyway. I picked some hair off his comb and mailed it in to this service I found online, and a couple weeks later, I get the envelope with the results — no paternal match. And . . . I didn't know what to do."

Even though I knew this story wasn't going to be ultimately sad, since this moment of paternity uncertainty was in the distant past, I felt like I should comfort her. I reached out and put my hand over hers. The sense of relief when she didn't pull away filled my whole body, and at least three-quarters of my soul.

"I walked around holding my breath for a week. I think I was looking for the perfect time to confess, or confront him, even though I don't think I had any idea what that moment would look like. And so, it happened without me deciding to. I was watching something on TV with my parents, and this cheesy commercial came on with this dad who's really nervous that his daughter's finally driving, and I just started bawling. Both my parents assumed there was something physically wrong with me, because eleven-year-olds don't normally get choked up watching Toyota commercials. They rushed over and started asking what was wrong, and kind of grabbing at limbs to check if there were any outward signs of whatever had just malfunctioned inside of me. And in between sobs I explained that I finally knew the horrible family secret, that my dad wasn't my dad, so he didn't have to pretend anymore. That I knew because I had stolen hair off Dad's brush and gotten the DNA results back. And then they both started laughing."

"That is . . . not the reaction I would have expected," I said.

"Yeah, not really what I was expecting either. I had uncovered a big family secret — my father had been mostly bald since before I was born. So the hair I plucked off the brush did come off my father's head, but not exactly from my father's head."

I tried to focus on the table, the small dent in the napkin holder, anything to stop thinking about Gwen's father's hairpiece, but I failed, and I started laughing, which, thank god, set Gwen off too.

"Were your parents mad?" I asked once I managed to get my laughter semi–under control. "I mean, there are some obvious implications about trying to find out your paternity if you think your mom is still your biological mom."

"We have successfully sidestepped any slut shaming implications to this very day," Gwen said, smiling. I had to add discussions of toupees and suspected adultery to the list of things that didn't even dampen my urge to kiss her.

"So, getting back to my point. Because I actually don't usually tell this story on a first date."

*Date!* The label hadn't really been up in the air, but it was still thrilling to hear her say it. And first implied a series, a saga, a collection of upcoming dates!

"I'm not saying me walking around with this huge question mark hanging over my family for a week is anything like what you've had to deal with. But I am saying that if you have even one percent of that nervous uncertainty, I think you should email the mystery cousin."

I pulled my hand out of hers, jerkily. I regretted it as soon as I did it, since I knew from countless TV shows and movies that this was the universal signal for *You've said the magic words and now I definitely don't want a romantic future with you.* But I just needed both my hands if I was going to think. Thinking that can't be done on the floor in full starfish at least requires some rapid thumb twirling.

"You don't know what I might find," I said, quietly.

"Neither do you. She could be great —"

"Not all family mysteries end as neatly as yours."

Gwen looked down. I could feel my throat tightening. For the second time in the space of two minutes, I had hacked at whatever deeper connection we were making. Why had I said that? It wasn't her fault she hadn't had been left behind. It wasn't her fault that she was lucky. And I was lucky, too. I shouldn't have had to remind myself of that so often.

"I'm sorry, I'm sorry, I didn't mean—"

"No, you're totally right. I tell a story about one week of not knowing something about my family, and . . . I have no idea what you're going through—"

"But I want you to."

I wished I were a musician or a poet or a sculptor or something so that I could capture Gwen's slowly spreading smile, or maybe just the feeling of it, of the sun finally peeking through the window in the middle of January, granting you a sensation of warmth that seemed so impossible just a minute before. Gwen's smile was like that—completely miraculous. "I want to, too," she said.

I was so busy basking in her glow, I forgot for a second what it was that we both wanted: for her to know what I was going through. Which meant I should also figure out what I was going through. And then explain it, out loud, in a restaurant that was playing, I realized, an acoustic version of "Cotton-Eyed Joe." I took a deep breath and let it out so dramatically, it made the wrapper from my straw skitter across the table.

"I love my parents. My parents love me. I should be grateful for that. I am grateful for that. And I guess having questions seems like . . . a betrayal."

I looked up at Gwen, who was looking at me with her full attention and no indication that she was going to do anything but listen.

"And I've just sat with them for so long, the questions, that all the crazy little-kid questions have gotten tangled up in the actual questions, so, in a way, breast cancer running in my family seems just as plausible as a witch's curse that won't reveal itself until the eve of my twenty-first birthday. I know, as a reasonable person, I should want to take steps to tackle both potential problems, but a big part of me would rather just not know."

I took another deep breath. I didn't think I had talked so long, uninterrupted, since the last time I gave an in-class presentation.

"I'm living two stories right now. The one that seems real and has a happy ending, or at least a happy middle—'Abandoned girl finds loving home.' But I know there's another one too: 'Baby born, baby left.' There is no happy ending to that story, just a sad, more fleshed-out middle. Happy, healthy, kind people don't leave their children in train stations. Something went wrong there. And without answers, it's just this vague floating thing that doesn't define me. 'Baby internet star' is a conversation starter. 'Girl thrown away by someone with a mental illness or addiction or who is a terrible person who got sick of their kid'—that's a box that I don't want to be put in. Instead, 'Baby grows up in loving home, grainy CCTV footage reveals no clues, one of the less reputable pages on Wikipedia is started. Life moves on.'"

I had never said that out loud—what I knew my bio mother or father or both must be. The fact that in my best daydreams they were sick and struggling. That the worst-case scenario for them was the best for me. I didn't like what that said about me.

"Janey, you don't have to go all the way to your birth parents. You said your adopted aunt is a dead end, right? This might be the safest way to rule out the witch's curse. Meet some bio family, get some answers, but not all the answers, if you don't want them," she said.

"We don't have to keep talking about this," I muttered. She was being so nice, but no one wants to get this deep into someone else's issues on a first date. This is the kind of story that pops up on a message board then goes viral. "I just wanted to share a plate of fries, she shared deeply held insecurities that stem from a childhood trauma."

"I don't mind. But we can talk about something else, if you want," she offered, putting her hand over mine again. I linked my fingers in between hers. I needed to stop thinking about that stupid acorn. The weight of it was crushing me, threatening to flatten every wonderful feeling holding hands with Gwen was giving me. I was in charge of my own mind, and I would decide what was making my heart race. I wished, for possibly the first time in my life, that I lived in the suburbs, somewhere teenagers had cars that they could park in shadowy spots with corny names and the kind of cafeteria table clique–busting solidarity that comes from a shared desire to make out undisturbed.

"Do you want to go to a movie?" I blurted out.

"Sure. What one?"

"What's actually playing . . . doesn't really matter . . ."

I couldn't look at her. It was the most brazenly forward line I had ever imagined, let alone said out loud. I was mildly terrified my complete absence of finesse might have been confusing, which would force me to clarify "because we'll be making out during the movie," and if I had to add that asterisk, I would die of embarrassment.

"Jane, are you asking me to make out with you in the back of a dark movie theater?" she asked. I thought I heard a smile in her voice, but I still couldn't bring myself to look up. No one called me *Jane*. I loved that I was someone new to her. I nodded. She slipped her hand out of mine, and I watched as she reached into her purse, pulled out a twenty, and put it in the center of the table.

"What about our milkshake?" I asked.

"Do you really care about the milkshake?" she asked.

I could only shake my head.

"Let's go."

Thirty minutes later we were sitting at the back of the dingiest AMC in Manhattan. She had let me pick, and I had gone with a horror movie involving some kind of man-eating demon bug. Not the most romantic atmosphere, but I figured if someone was getting their face eaten off in Dolby surround sound, our fellow moviegoers were less likely to notice a pair of teenagers completely uninterested in the carnage.

We held hands, fingers laced, and even though being linked to Gwen still felt electric, it was also beginning to feel natural. Like this was where my hand belonged. I could take only little shallow breaths through all the credits, nervous that more movement could inspire some kind of shift to make her let go. Then the lights went all the way down, and a misty forest filled the screen.

"You know what's really the scariest part of those woods?" I asked, whispering in her ear.

"What?"

"The threat of Lyme disease."

It turned out that my only move was directness couched in

extreme awkwardness and bad jokes. But it must have worked because I had barely invoked tick-borne illness when Gwen's lips moved to mine. Thank god I hadn't put down the armrest. Gwen was a very good kisser, I thought. How could you separate someone's actual kissing skills from the thrill of the person you've dreamed about kissing you actually doing it?

As a blood-curdling scream filled the theater, Gwen moved from my mouth to my neck, which I hadn't even realized was a possible venue change before last night and yet was quickly becoming my absolute favorite venue change. Gwen created an endless line of lips and tongue from my jaw to my clavicle, which was interesting, because it felt like those might be the only bones left in my body. The rest had liquified, or maybe emulsified? There was definitely fire involved, but the process was anything but unpleasant. It was somehow even more intense than last night, whether it was because we had opened up to each other or the distant screams bouncing around us in Dolby surround sound made the make-out session seem deliciously desperate. If this was my last moment on earth before I was devoured by a giant man-size bug, it was exactly how I'd want to be spending it. And suddenly I really needed her to know that.

"I've wanted to kiss you for a really, really long time. And this is so much better than any daydream I ever had," I whispered, making sure not to drop my gaze. The crunch of bones being crushed erupted in the theater as a flash of light from the screen illuminated her face. She was so beautiful, but that wasn't even what I was thinking about. I was thinking about how many times I could have scared her off earlier at the restaurant. But she had stayed.

"Then that's what we'll do," she whispered, "Kiss for a really, really long time."

Her deliberate misreading of my confession, the pivot into corny word play, was almost sexier than anything that had happened so far. Almost.

The movie was way too short. It seemed like we had just gotten there when the lights came back up and Gwen and I had to leave row Z, seats 24 and 25, the best movie seats in the history of the world. Gwen's hair was a little messed up, but it somehow seemed even better, like each curl had ended up where it was meant to be. Her cheeks were a little red, and her lips were even redder. It made me think of Snow White — "lips as red as a rose." I wondered if Snow White had been described after she had been making out for ninety-five minutes, too.

"I had a really good time," I said as we stood outside the theater, Gwen getting ready to go left to take the train uptown to Algie's, me getting ready to turn right. "A really good time" seemed like an almost criminal understatement.

"Me too." She smiled, squeezing my hand.

"We should . . . do this again sometime."

"Which part?" she asked. And she pulled me toward her and kissed me, on the sidewalk, in front of tourists and moms and someone handing out pamphlets, which is so different from kissing in the back of a movie theater. It was half kiss, half proclamation — *This is someone I like kissing, and I don't care who knows it.*

"I'll text you later," she called over her shoulder as she walked toward the subway. I watched her until she disappeared around a corner. I fought the urge to run through every rom-com cliché. I wanted to gently touch my lips, remembering where they had just been. I wanted to sigh and collapse into the wall. I wanted to jump up and down and do a kind of silent scream and then spin in a circle with my arms outstretched. And I loved my city because I knew I could do any combination of those things and absolutely no one would even pause to look at me. But instead, I dialed Algie's number, because there was no way I could express what I was feeling in a text — even with reaction GIFs at my disposal.

"So, are you a Fairfax yet?" Algie asked as soon as he picked up. I considered questioning what made him think I'd take her last name, but I was too excited to start that kind of debate.

"Not yet. Although I think we've made some solid progress in that direction."

By three a.m., some, but not all, of the afternoon's glow had worn off. Gwen did text me, as promised, and said good night around one. It was incredible to have someone to say good night to. But that left two hours to stare at the Instagram handle Algie had finally sent me (of course when I wasn't in any state to emotionally multitask). S_Snoot. Not terribly creative. I'd looked at it so long, the S_S had started to look like a bored emoticon with deconstructed dollar-sign eyes. Or maybe someone so in love with the letter S, they'd gone slightly catatonic.

I realized I had been giving my full attention to the handle much longer than was healthy, and that before I started scripting a miniseries about the S-eyed man and his quest for letter love, I had to make a decision: to open Pandora's box, or not. Or Pandora's jar, if you're going to be true to the original myth. Which I tried to be.

I started to hum the *Jeopardy!* theme song. I tapped on the message icon. I began to type a message to my biological cousin. My first three attempts came out as a barely readable jumble of typos. But by the fourth draft, I wrote something that was at least coherent:


Dear Sandra,

I understand this message might seem weird, or made up, like I'm a prince asking for money, but I promise it's not a scam. I recently got one of those DNA tests, and I found out we're actually first cousins, which makes sense, I mean it makes sense that we've never met, because I'm adopted. And recently I've gotten curious about meeting some of my biological relatives. I know this might not be something you're interested in, which I would totally respect and not bother you again. But I saw in your bio that you're in Jersey City, and I'm in Astoria, and those are two places that are fairly close to each other. So, if you were interested in meeting up, it wouldn't be hard. Geographically.

Sincerely,

J.W.


I considered a bunch of different sign-offs. *Your long-lost cousin* sounded too cheesy, or like I was writing in to an advice column. My full name was too googleable, and I wanted to actually talk to Sandra before revealing my use of *I'm adopted* didn't really give an accurate picture of my full origin story. I decided on *J.W.,* which seemed like a nickname used by a guy, and all those studies show that when an email is signed with a guy's name, it gets more respect and attention, so maybe that would help. I hit Send and listened to the whooshing sound of my message rocketing toward Sandra. Even though I knew she was probably asleep, I stayed up for another few hours, watching videos of animals making friends with different types of animals, refreshing my inbox every time a dog gave a cat a hug.

# CHAPTER SIX

**It takes a great deal of courage to see the world in all its
tainted glory, and still to love it.**

–OSCAR WILDE, *AN IDEAL HUSBAND*

It was kind of nice to know that even at eighteen years old, there were things I could still learn about myself. Like, for example, that when my entire body was simultaneously consumed by crippling anxiety and incredible joy, my skin seemed to tingle with static electricity. I pictured the two forces colliding like a hot and cold front, sparking lightning.

"I think I might be finally getting my superpower," I whispered to Algie, his entire focus on the clay cat in front of him as he hash marked its muddy back with an X-ACTO knife.

"Excellent. Happy for you. But unless it's heat vision you can use to save me from the kiln line, I'm not interested right now," he said.

Spring break had passed in a blur of staring with painful intensity at my phone waiting for a message from Sandra that never came and a new text from Gwen, which came with amazing regularity. *She* was actually the one who'd started a countdown to a bowling double date planned for this coming Tuesday night with Algie and Cecil. Her texts were fast and funny. And, yes, sometimes they stopped abruptly and would come back hours later, leaving me, during those long pauses, convinced I would never hear from her again. At least being back in class meant I was separated for a few hours from my screen and the stress of decoding the many possible layers of subtext in Gwen's every emoji use. I hadn't told Algie about the message to Sandra Snoot. Or Gwen. Or Cecil. Or my parents. I didn't want anyone else to know I had somehow courted even more rejection from my biological family.

Senior year art class was never really a class so much as art therapy to prevent a collective breakdown from the stress of our other classes. Even so, the closer we got to graduation, the more we seemed to be regressing. At least three girls headed to West Coast schools had insisted on working on ashtrays for their parents, "to remember us when we're gone."

When Ms. Rajotte asked Kelsey if her parents smoked, she said no, but then added with legitimate wistfulness, "When they look at this, they'll remember that I never gave in to peer pressure." Algie didn't even try to hide his giggles, well aware that absolutely no one had ever offered Kelsey a cigarette in her life, but that she was basically addicted to grotesquely bloated vodka-soaked gummy bears.

I had started to add toothpick-etched flowers along the edge of my pinch pot when I heard the familiar squelching sound of another one of Algie's creations hitting the floor in defeat. I didn't look up right away — it's important to let Algie work for my attention a little bit. But I was glad that our school didn't have the budget for a chem lab, or I felt like we'd both be graduating with fewer toes than we started with.

"I'm meeting Cecil today," he said. I jerked my head up to see him smiling wickedly as he rolled a new piece of clay into a red-brown log/ worm/unappetizing piece of spaghetti.

"That is a terrible idea. In fact, I forbid it," I said, hoping I sounded forceful and possibly a little intimidating. I'd assumed their next date would be our double date, meaning I'd be able to supervise to make sure Algie was being (somewhat) nice and Cecil remained (kind of) clear-eyed about Algie.

"That's adorable, Janey," he said, adding half-moon eyes and a smile with his thumbnail to his worm/very friendly piece of spaghetti.

"What are you doing? Where are you going?"

"Who was that man I saw you with last night?! Answer me!" Algie interrupted me in his best "wife from a made-for-TV movie" voice.

"God, JJ, you act like I'm taking a hit out on him or something. I simply invited your cousin to join me in the park for a picnic. Your cousin, who, may I remind you, is also my prom date? The picture of innocence," he said.

"I'm coming with you."

"I don't think he needs a chaperone."

"You need a chaperone. I'll bring brownies."

Algie sighed and put his clay friend on the shoulder of his suit jacket, which up until this moment, had been completely free of art class debris (my white tank top was so splattered, it looked like a before picture in a detergent ad).

"Fine. You can crash. I guess I'll just have to work a little harder to set the mood with a third wheel dragging everything down," he said.

I pulled out my cell phone. No new texts from Gwen, but four from Cecil. I knew I shouldn't check my Insta messages, but I did. Still nothing from Sandra. I opened Cecil's texts.

> Meeting Algernon in the park-what is he into, btw? Need to work on talking points.

> Should I bring my own picnic blanket?

> Should I be a little late? Do you think he'd think that's rude, or intriguing? Would you describe me as intriguing? Could you, to Algie?

> I know my dragon T-shirt is kind of dorky, but it kind of makes me look like that guy on the CW. Do you think it's worth it?

> Chill, Cecil. I'm crashing your date.

That's awesome. I mean. You probably don't have to crash the whole thing. But just the start would be great.

---

## CECIL CARDEW, DEFENDER OF ROMANCE AND WHALES

Cecil Cardew was born two months early both adorably and dangerously small, as he would remain relative to the size and danger of the ever-changing world for the rest of his life. Cardew's ambitions were simple yet daunting, as he outlined in a kind of manifesto one rainy day in the sixth grade while hanging out with his cousin — "True love everlasting."

He had heard the phrase on some kind of fantasy romance show his babysitter at the time was watching, and instantly he knew that was all he wanted from life.

Recognizing this was a self-centered life goal, Mr. Cardew always took pains to encourage true love everlasting to bloom in the lives of those around him. Sometimes this meant friends and family. Often, it was simply directed at strangers he believed he could nudge toward true happiness by playing love songs on the subway just low enough that people could hear something, but not loud enough to confirm it wasn't a ringtone or the squeal of the tracks or to actually inspire anything. After finding the love of his life and settling into marriage, Cardew spent the rest of his days working on his conservation efforts to save the whales. He continues to survive with his husband, who only smiles adoringly every time Cardew reads a new Modern Love column at the kitchen table and audibly sighs with happiness.

———————

Algie was wearing a cravat. Algie, like all people who are not, at this moment, acting in a period piece, looked ridiculous in a cravat. His ridiculousness was magnified by the fact he'd paired his cravat with a long cigarette holder, which he was using to spear pretzel rods from a bag.

"Why?" I asked, out of habit more than an actual desire to get to the bottom of his fashion choices.

"It's a power play, Janey. When Cecil sees how hot I look even in less than flattering accessories, he'll be able to imagine just how amazing I'd look when dressed in a more traditional, Gen Z post-Abercrombie prep ensemble. And it's that imagination that will really keep him coming back for more," Algie said, biting the end off of a pretzel.

"My baby cousin," I whined.

"Stop infantilizing him, Janey. It'll do nothing to prepare him for the world — neither its dangers, nor its pleasures."

"Jesus, when you say *pleasures,* it sounds even grosser than *moist.*"

"It won't when you're older, JJ, and have also experienced true pleasure. It's like that old Christmas book where you stop hearing the sleigh bells when you stop believing in Santa. Once you realize just what it feels like, you'll only be able to hear the beauty in the word. But then again, you have experienced true pleasure, haven't you? Have I said a word about you sticking your tongue down my cousin's throat when good, god-fearing Americans were trying to enjoy *DemonBug: The Resurrection?*"

"You have said so many words about it."

"But only words of encouragement. Someday I hope you'll be just as supportive as I am. And we're here," Algie said as we hit the stage. The stage was actually a rec room–size concrete slab rising a few feet out of the weeds in an otherwise unremarkable part of the park, but it was still the best place to picnic if you wanted to avoid ants and used needles. Algie spread out the blanket, and I started unpacking various vending machine pouches when I heard Cecil call from down the hill.

"Hey, guys!"

Cecil was wearing what I knew were his best jeans, paired with the actual Supreme T-shirt my parents got him for Christmas last year. And he was looking at Algie with all the wonder he'd pull out for an honest-to-god cast member of *Riverdale.*

As we all sat down, Cecil turned toward me, not the object of his mental undressing. He probably read on some Tumblr thread that you shouldn't be too thirsty on the first date. Of course, Cecil was in a constant state of thirst, but there was really no way for me to tell him to tone it down in front of his date.

"So, Cecil," Algie said, "what's your best story?"

"My what?" Cecil kind of bleated, and looked at me accusingly, like it was my job to prep him.

"Your story. You know, that one you're always dying to tell strangers, just looking for the smallest connection in whatever they're saying so you can interrupt them with your obviously more interesting monologue. I've discovered it's easier to just get those out of the way. Plus, if someone's best story is actually kind of the worst, you know to keep your expectations low," Algie said as he tied the legs of two gummy octopi together.

"Jesus, Algie. Why not just tell him he's going to be scored on a scale of one to five? And if he isn't at least a level-three interesting, he's so not getting college credit?" I asked, in a tone I hoped conveyed the depth of my disapproval.

Cecil stared at his phone like he was willing it to produce his own personal *Game of Thrones*–level saga, scrolling with a raw kind of desperation.

"Cecil, I'm looking for an original story. I keep up on what Reddit has to offer as far as glimpses into the collective psyche. Although, I guess I could use a dramatic reading—"

"Sorry, I just—" Cecil interrupted. "I'm scanning my diary."

"You keep a diary?" Algie asked at the same time I said, "On your phone?"

I remembered Cecil's stacks of marbled notebooks from middle school, hidden not so stealthily under his mattress and filled with, according to his twelve-year-old self, "only the greatest hidden secrets of my soul. And some pretty awesome Yu-Gi-Oh! sketches."

"Of course I keep a diary," Cecil said with a shy smile. "How else would I remember my life otherwise? Plus, it's kind of motivating to not be boring, you know? It's one thing to do nothing all day, but when you have to actually write it down, relive your nothingness, it kind of makes you want to try skydiving the next day, just so whoever digs it out of an attic or cyberspace in a hundred years won't get bored, you know?"

I glanced at Algie, who was looking at Cecil with a little more interest.

"So, did you find something? A story so compelling, we won't even think about checking our phones halfway through, even if we get a notification?" Algie asked. I rolled my eyes. If Algie ever ignored a buzz against his leg, I'd know for sure he had been body snatched. And on some days, I thought I'd wait to see how much easier life with the body snatcher would be before I started planning the rescue mission.

"I have one," Cecil suddenly shouted, and I realized in empathic horror that he was actually raising his hand.

"I'm not calling on you," Algie said, smiling at Cecil like he was one of those tiny fainting goats — helpless but somehow adorable.

Cecil's blush was so extreme it invaded his forehead, but he managed a weak smile before launching into his best story.

"So, this one time, in fourth grade, we had a pet hamster —"

"I'm already marking this down for lack of originality. Pet

misfortunes are overdone. In sitcoms, in teary confessions on reality shows. Tell it to me straight, Cecil. Did you kill your class hamster?"

"What? No. I'm pretty sure Mr. Gerbil is still alive."

"Mr. —"

"They look pretty much the same and we weren't given enough information before the naming."

"Okay. I'm slightly intrigued. Slightly. You may proceed," Algie said, bunching up his jacket into a pillow before lying down on the slab, probably trying to temper that heap of praise with a little calculated disinterest.

"So, anyway. We had a class hamster, Mr. Gerbil, and this girl in my class, Gabby, started crying, like, as soon as Ms. M. brought him out. And not like loud, look-at-me crying. Just a totally quiet rain of tears and snot. It was freaky. And Ms. M. kept asking her if she was afraid and if she wanted to leave the room, and Gabby kept saying 'No, no, no,' but she still continued crying. And you know, you can't be a teacher and just order a ten-year-old to stop crying unless you're a monster, so Ms. M. just kind of, like, let her be. So, we put Mr. Gerbil's cage aside and went back to, like, math or whatever, and Gabby's still crying. At lunch, Gabby always sat at the end of my table, so I went over. I think I thought that I could offer her some animal crackers or something to cheer her up. And I go over there, and she's just eating yogurt and still crying, like, actively. You know how you'll see a really little kid, like, at the end of a cry, kind of hiccupping and eating? This was like blink, new tears, spoon full of strawberry banana, repeat. I wasn't even really thinking about helping her anymore. I was just so, like, horrified and entranced, and so I just go, 'Gabby, why are you crying?' which, by the way, no one had asked. Like, it coincided with Mr. Gerbil, but for all we knew, she had snuck a peek at her phone and just found out her grandma died or whatever, but she just looks up at me so, so sadly and goes, 'He'll never run in the sun, Cecil,' and she went back to her yogurt. And I was just, like, I didn't even know swears then, because we didn't have HBO yet, but whatever the, like, little kid version of *shit, man* is, that's what went through my head. We went back to the classroom and she eventually stopped crying and the school year carried on, and we gave Mr. Gerbil extra carrots for Christmas. When we had elementary school graduation, he got a little graduation cap, but Gabby was right. He never ran in the sun."

Cecil looked down as he finished, and I looked at Algie to gauge his reaction to whatever Cecil was trying to say. I was waiting for the burn, the zing, something biting that probably had to do with the combo of E. B. White and Tim Burton vibes the story had, when I heard Algie whisper, "That's actually a pretty good story, Cecil. Needs an epilogue, though."

"I told you, I think he's still alive —"

"Not the hamster. Gabby."

"Oh. She moved in seventh grade. I wasn't on Instagram then, so I don't know. But I have her quote written down in a bunch of places on one of the walls of my room, on most of my notebooks. I think it's kind of cool, actually. That she'll probably never know that at least by one person, she's quotable. She's immortalized," Cecil said.

"I think you might be overestimating the lifespan of your room and notebooks. And yourself, actually. But I like that kind of oversize ego in a guy," Algie said, tossing Cecil a bag of chips that didn't even come close to reaching him. He waited until Cecil scooted over and started to grab the bag before pretending to "assist," him, putting his hand over Cecil's. It was a middle school (if you went to middle school in the '50s) move and I was about to laugh out loud when I saw Cecil's expression of open wonder. The poor guy didn't just have heart eyes, he had heart entire-goddamn face. And I really didn't want to spoil it for him. Maybe I was worrying over nothing. Maybe Cecil would be the one to convince Algie to have an actual relationship.

"Uh, guys, I forgot. I have to finish a book report," I said, getting up kind of gingerly to make sure I didn't burst the romantic bubble I had just watched descend over them.

"Jesus, Janey, you are the world's worst liar. We haven't had to do a book report in a decade," Algie said, eyes still on Cecil.

"It's not for school. It's, uh, for my parents. You know, something Mom saw on the *Today* show. Connect with your teens through family reading and stuff. Anyway. Two hundred words on *To Kill a Mockingbird* or no dessert."

"You only have to lie if the people being ditched don't want to be, Janey," Algie said, finally looking up at me and grinning. "Cecil and I are completely fine with you fleeing. But leave the Fruit Roll-Ups."

As I walked away, I felt my phone buzz in my pocket and saw a red notification dotting my Instagram app. I opened it up and stared down at one message. From Sandra.

Hi Janey,

I'm so sorry it took me so long to write back! Things have been crazy at work, but it's so nice to hear from you! Anyway, I'm sorry if this is a little creepy, haha, but I looked up the school in your Insta bio and realized it's downtown NYC, which is actually where my mom lives! Small world, right? Or maybe big world, but energy always flowing back to the center (can you tell I work in a meditation center yet?!). Anyway, she'd love to meet you, if you're interested. I know you wanted to know about your birth parents, and I just wanted to, I don't know, warn you that my mom had a bad experience trying to look for her birth parents a long time ago, so I don't think you'll get any info from her. But you could get an aunt, which is great. My aunt took me to get my tongue pierced when I was fifteen, and my other aunt took me to the walk-in clinic after it got infected. I'm very pro-aunt. Anyway, let me know if you want to meet up with my mom, and we should hang out sometime, too. How do you feel about salt caves?

Talk to you later, cuz!

– Sandra

I had to sit down on the ground for a second, and once I was far away enough from the slab that Algie wouldn't accuse me of spying, I sat on the grass, reading and rereading the message. My cousin wanted to hang out. She was funny, and kind of ramble-y, like me.

Maybe it ran in the family. Maybe it ran in my family. I wanted to write back that I had no idea what salt caves were, but if that was where she wanted to hang out, I was more than willing to check them out. I wanted to write that my aunt, Cecil's mom, once got me a ticket to a Museum of Natural History sleepover, and even when the museum people told us we needed to stay in the room with all the cots, she snuck me into the fossils exhibit and made up names for all the different dinosaurs. Another one of my aunts, who lived in Arizona and I'd only seen a handful of times, bought me a beautiful leather journal for my sixteenth birthday with a card that said, "A book worthy of all your wonderful thoughts." But all of that seemed like maybe too much information to saddle Sandra with at the outset. Maybe these were stories I'd tell her in person when I could see her expression. So instead, I sent back the simplest possible reply:

> Hi Sandra,
>
> It's so great to hear from you. I don't think it's creepy that you looked up my school. I'm glad you found a connection in the maybe small, maybe energy-filled world. I'd love to meet up with your mom sometime. Let me know when she's free.
>
> – Janey

I hit Send and listened for the whoosh, then I was up and wiping the bits of grass off my jeans. I smiled all through my subway ride, no matter what noises or smells entered the car. I was going to meet my biological aunt. And then maybe my biological cousin. I was going to meet people who looked like me and maybe had answers for me. Sitting in a mostly deserted car, I looked at my latest text from Gwen.

Can't wait to see you tomorrow night at bowling!

It was possible I was getting good at not scaring people away.

# CHAPTER SEVEN

**One should always be a little improbable.**

−OSCAR WILDE

Algie and I arrived outside the bowling alley almost at the same moment, and he decided it would be best to wait outside for Gwen, in case the laser show constantly happening inside Pins and Spins left her too disoriented to recognize her favorite cousin and most recent lover (his words, definitely not mine).

I leaned against the building, then thought better of it and straightened up.

"So, I kind of made a coffee date with my long-lost aunt. In a week," I said, choosing to look down so I wouldn't have to deal with Algie's expression and his answer.

"That seems like enough time for you to have multiple crises. Can we schedule them in now so I can plan?" Algie quipped.

"Yes, act like I'm the more high-maintenance friend. I at least know that at three a.m. the average person is sleeping and thus probably not in the right state of mind to help someone else rank the desirability of the lacrosse team."

"Oh, but Janey, I know you're not the average person —"

"I agree," Gwen said, seeming to materialize around the corner.

I offered her a smile that felt like the kind of violent squiggle lovestruck mouths make in old-timey cartoons.

The three of us stepped into the building and took in the sights and sounds together. The whole place seemed like it has been preserved in amber, every noise and smell and health code violation exactly the same as when my parents used to take me and Cecil when we were little kids and he visited the city—before I fully understood the bacterial implications of putting on someone else's shoes and before Cecil got really into soccer. Algie, Gwen, and I were still considering our footwear options when Cecil showed up, eyes bright, bowling shirt brighter.

"A bold choice, Cecil. I applaud your ability to stand out, even in the most neon of settings," Algie said, in a way that seemed mean enough that I wanted to call him out, if it weren't so obvious his venom was meant to be flirty. Using insults to flirt was part of a larger conversation I'd been having with him since sixth grade that I didn't particularly want to get into amidst the clouds of hot dog and nacho fumes.

"So, are you any good?" Gwen asked, taking my hand and lacing her fingers with mine, an impressive feat considering my entire hand seemed to have a mini-convulsion at her touch.

"I'm not bad with the bumpers on," I whispered. At this point, I wasn't even attempting to sexy whisper. I just worried I might lose all control of vocal volume and figured it was better to err on the softer side.

"Well, I'm actually pretty great. If there's a direct transfer of skills from Wii bowling to actual bowling," she said.

Her hair was pinned to the side with a long silver barrette that showed off a drop earring, a shimmering purple stone almost brushing her shoulder. I tried to focus on it, putting all my energy into the purple orb in the hope that focusing somewhere Gwen adjacent rather than directly on Gwen's face would up my chances of behaving like an actual human being tonight. I really had thought that after you make out with someone in the movies, the butterflies in your stomach might chill the heck out. But I was rapidly realizing that I might have felt even more nervous about screwing up and losing what I had with Gwen right then than when having something with Gwen had only been a fantasy.

After our shoes had been selected and Lysoled (twice, by my request), Cecil announced it was time to pick team names.

"I think we need to pick teams first," Gwen said.

"Let's do guys versus girls," Cecil suggested, sounding as nervous as I felt.

"Gender is a construct. I vote we team up with whoever we'd most like to kiss when they get a strike," Gwen suggested.

"Seconded," Algie agreed, before giving Cecil an incredibly chaste peck on the check that turned his entire face almost alarmingly red. It was such a PG moment, I wondered if Algie actually had been listening to my pleas to tread carefully when it came to my cousin's heart.

"Any suggestions?" Gwen, my now official teammate, asked as she stood over the keyboard, the old-school blinking green cursor on the screen in front of her mirrored on the TV mounted above the lane. Our first public display of unity, first joint project, first chance to shout from the rooftop, or even the vaulted ceiling of the bowling alley, that Gwen and I were at least temporarily Gwen and me.

"End Game," I said, practically involuntarily.

I froze. *End game?!* That was what stalkers said on the second date. And this wasn't even a second single date. It was a double date, a date that comes with even fewer romantic expectations. I desperately reached for an explanation that would convince her that I hadn't been collecting her discarded bubblegum to turn into a closet shrine.

"Like, as soon as the other team sees us, they know it's, like, the end of the game. They might as well go home now. Not even bother warming up . . ." I trailed off.

The phrase I was describing, of course, was *game over,* not *end game.* I held my breath, waiting for Gwen to call me out on either my incredibly too soon romantic declaration or my inability to remember idiomatic English. Instead, she just smiled.

"I like it. Finality before we begin." She typed it in, then sat down as Cecil, still slightly pink, typed in the even more devastatingly embarrassing *Ballers.* ("If anyone tries to tie me to that name beyond tonight, I will deny it," Algie shouted.)

Gwen, as it turned out, was good at bowling. She was also good at gracefully spinning toward me after her ball had connected with the pins, which created a satisfying sound that was the only thing I really missed about this place.

"So, what are we going to do to celebrate when we win?" she asked, sitting next to me on the bench after getting a spare. I fingered the end of my braid, some kind of elaborate basket weave Gwen had managed in less time than it took for Algie to bowl his third gutter ball.

"We could see a movie?" I suggested, forcing myself to keep eye contact. Her perfectly shaped eyebrows shot up as she smiled.

"Another horror one, you think?"

"I do love horror."

"I hadn't been a big horror fan before, but I'm really starting to like the genre."

I wrapped my arm around her waist and kissed her, hard, right there in the bowling alley. I pulled away at the sound of Algie's applause, but I didn't turn toward him. I kept my eyes on Gwen, who kept her eyes on me. I felt a little of that nervousness mercifully melt away. Not because I wasn't still terrified of Gwen leaving, but because my happiness was crowding out any other conflicting emotions. I almost forgot we were still technically in the middle of a game.

"Janey. It's your turn. Please bowl quickly so you can end this with merciful swiftness," Algie said, putting his arm on the table followed by his head in a sign of utter defeat that could only mean he had just put another gutter ball onto the scoreboard while Gwen and I had been . . . not paying attention.

Before I could even grab my ball, a child's screech ripped through the bowling alley. I turned to see a little boy in orange overalls, maybe five years old, carrying a bowling ball that looked like it was literally half his size. He was running with practically supernatural speed away from a very tired-looking woman who furiously whisper-yelled, "Ben!" as she ran after him.

"I don't want to give it back. I like my ball. It's orange! It's my ball," Ben shouted as he careened toward us. I don't think the kid had a violent plan. I really don't think he was aiming for anyone, as mad as he was at the universe for trying to take away a ball that so perfectly matched his outfit. But whatever his intentions, the actuality was this —just as Algie was bringing his head up to see what was making the horrible noise, the tiny orange-clad boy somehow hoisted his equally orange ball onto the table, where it made violent contact with two of Algie's fingers that were resting halfway off the edge. Suddenly the boy went quiet, possibly because his orange ball was now slightly less orange, splattered with Algie's blood, and then he was screaming and running into his mother's arms as we all stared at Algie's hand in horror.

"I can see my bone" was all Algie whispered when I reached him and looked at his ring finger, which was already red and sticky but clearly had a bit of snapped white bone peeking out from the torn skin.

"Algie, breathe," Cecil commanded, appearing on Algie's other side with his bowling shirt in his hands.

"I'm going to wrap this around your hand so you can stop seeing it, but if I try to tie it off to stop the bleeding, I'm afraid I might cause more of a tear, so I need you to keep your arm above your head. Can you do that for me?" Cecil asked an increasingly pale-looking Algie, who looked from Cecil to me to Gwen, who looked almost as pale as Algie, but did not move to raise his arm.

"I should call 911," I said, digging in my purse.

"No, I saw an urgent care literally next door. We'll go there. Algie, can you stand?" Cecil asked. I looked at Cecil's shirt, already dip-dyed mostly red, and Algie's face, which had the kind of death pallor I had seen him get only after drinking large portions of his parent's wine cabinet.

"Okay, here we go," Cecil said. I was about to ask what the plan was when Cecil, who was at least two inches shorter and thirty pounds lighter than Algie, scooped him up and looped Algie's bloodied arm over his shoulder then rested the mangled hand on his head like the world's creepiest hat.

I took my eyes off them only for a second, to check on Gwen, who had managed to get off the bench, but still looked shaky.

"You don't like blood?" I asked.

"I love blood. Very useful. I just like it to stay where I can't see it," she explained with the ghost of a smile, eyes still fixed on my cousin's retreating feet.

"All right, we're fine and we're moving," said Cecil as he speed walked to the door.

I followed behind them, staring at Algie's face to make sure he knew I was there and while not as helpful practically, I was very present for emotional support. His eyes were unfocused, but then he sleepily blinked and made eye contact.

"This was in one of your movies," he said weakly. I didn't get the chance to tell him which rom-com he was thinking of, though, before he threw up all down Cecil's back. Cecil didn't break his stride, even as he must have felt the sick wetness seeping through his T-shirt, and just called over his shoulder to ask me, "He all right?" before pushing out the door. It was possibly the most romantic thing I had ever seen.

It was hard to think of Algie as lucky when the last I saw him, Cecil was carrying him back into an exam room, both of them covered in a rather impressive mix of vomit and blood. But getting rushed into the back of an urgent care center in midtown Manhattan without any wait time seems like even if the gods aren't actually smiling down on you, they are at least giving you a weak thumbs up. Gwen had her hands on her knees as we sat waiting for Algie to get his finger splinted and sewn up. I wasn't sure how to break the silence, or if she was even in the mood to talk. I wanted to put my hand on hers, which seemed like it should be okay, seeing as she instigated some hand-holding before and was more than accepting of a kiss. But it still felt opportunistic in a gross way, like I'd be using Algie's injury to get closer to her.

"Your cousin was impressive," Gwen whispered finally, keeping her eyes on the floor.

"He was, wasn't he? I've never seen him like that before. One time I was playing at his house as a kid and a neighbor got a bloody nose, and he fainted, like, instantly."

"Well, it's got to be the car thing," she said, looking up at me and smiling. I smiled back, even though I had no idea what she was talking about.

"I have no idea what you're talking about." Her smile had the power to turn off the moat I pictured between my thoughts and what actually came out of my mouth; the moat barrier had become a direct, brain-to-mouth log flume.

"You know, how parents can lift cars off their children, because of adrenaline and love? Cecil's complete infatuation with Algernon obviously gave him the temporary ability to be cool in a time of crisis."

"Love-activated superpowers. I like that idea," I said.

"Ever gotten any superpowers?" she asked. Her left hand moved from her knee to mine.

"Yes, but never through love, only through genetics," I pointed out.

Have you ever had your own words punch you in the gut? As soon as I said it, the now-familiar spinning wheel of questions about my bio family roared to life, but with fun add-ons like "What if I came from a family of superheroes and I was only abandoned for my own protection, à la Clark Kent?" Or "What if I came from a family with an unhealthy relationship between what's real and what isn't and I was originally named after a superhero, like Nicholas Cage's kid, Kal-El?" As my meeting with my bio aunt got closer (just a week away, my calendar app had reminded me this morning), it brought questions I had tried to stuff down for a really long time to the surface. I wondered if I should write them all down before we met up. I wondered what would happen if my aunt couldn't answer any of them either.

"I'm embarrassed," Gwen said, jolting me out of my own thoughts.

"Of what?" I asked, a little incredulous that she could be embarrassed by anything.

"I wasn't very helpful. Algie is one of the few people I actually really care about, and I sat there through his medical emergency."

She hadn't taken her hand off my knee, so I put my hand over hers and squeezed. She squeezed my knee. I lightly knocked my foot against her shoe. We were a Rube Goldberg machine of tactile comfort.

"Like you said, Cecil had it covered, right? Sometimes the best thing you can do is recognize when someone's handling a crisis and get out of their way," I said.

"But I want to be the one who takes charge. I mean, that just makes me sound like a control freak. I want to be someone . . . someone who's counted on," she explained.

"Me too," I said. Without thinking about it, I put my head on her shoulder. I didn't give myself time to freak out about the possible implications. When I felt her sigh, then relax, I relaxed too.

"Did Algie tell you I'm going to major in social work?"

"No," I said, relaxing into her a little more.

"I promise I didn't copy you. You can check my future plans essay from sophomore year. Anyway, my mother was completely horrified. 'A profession for other people' is what she called it. I ended up having to convince her that I'm really going for art history."

"Why social work?" I asked.

"You first," she said.

"Well . . . I have, like, no memories of being Bag Baby, right? My world starts in my house with my dad and my unshakable sense of stability and safety. But when my parents started telling me the story, and I started looking through some of the old newspaper clips, I realized there were these people who made sure I was okay before that. There were people who made sure my dad was actually a good guy, but more importantly, my dad told me this story about this one social worker, Bethany, who really stood up for him, wrote this completely beautiful letter about why he should get custody. This woman, who I have no memory of and who didn't know me, was responsible for giving me my family. I guess I want to help kids like that."

I was monologuing. I had unleashed a soliloquy onto Gwen, and for one horrifying second of eerie silence, I thought she might have fallen asleep.

"You must have written a really good admission essay," she said, and as I sat up, I saw her grin.

"To be fair, I had some really good source material. Okay. Your turn," I said.

Gwen pulled out her silver clip, letting her hair fall over her face, just for a moment, before bending forward, grabbing every single brown strand in her left hand and pulling them into a high ponytail. She looked determined and beautiful.

"I want to be useful. I haven't really done that yet. In eighteen years, I've been cute and polite for the most part and sometimes clever, when it suits me. But I haven't really helped anyone or the planet. My school doesn't even have a can drive or a coat drive. I could have found one on my own, or even started one, but I didn't. And as you can see, I can't be a doctor or a nurse, and I don't think I'm going to invent anything important. So I bought all these career books and took quizzes and watched mini-YouTube documentaries. Then I did this career exploration interview with a social worker freshman year, and I think I'll be able to make up for these first eighteen years really fast," she said.

"I think it's possible you helped people and didn't even know it. That just your Gwen-ness was enough, and living with it your whole life, you didn't notice the effect," I said.

Gwen was quiet for a moment.

"Do you think he'll have a scar?" she asked, looking toward the hall where the guys disappeared forever ago, but according to my phone was only actually twenty minutes.

"Hopefully. You know how Algie feels about scars," I reminded her, smiling, thinking about how jealous he was of Andy M.'s appendix scar in fifth grade. Then years later in eighth grade, when I was attempting to cover the one on my ankle with concealer, he explained scars were concrete proof you had at least one good story.

"I live!" Algie's voice suddenly echoed through the halls. He emerged, still pale but more alert looking, his finger sporting a silver and blue foam splint. He was wearing a mint-green paper gown over his jeans and was followed by Cecil, also wearing a gown (and both were still in their rented bowling shoes). They looked like patients conspiring to break out of a hospital together.

"A trendsetter no matter the situation, cuz?" Gwen said, standing and looking Algie up and down, then Cecil.

"You okay, Algie?" I asked.

"Janey, we are never going bowling again. I can't believe my blood has been shed on pizza-pattern carpet. I am ashamed. I am maimed. I want Chipotle and pain killers, right now. Someone call a Lyft," he demanded, before collapsing in the closest chair to the door.

Gwen started typing as she walked toward Algie. I caught Cecil leaning against the wall, looking very small in the paper gown.

"C? That was pretty amazing. I think you might have a future as an EMT," I said, wondering whether he'd notice if a reassuring pat on the arm casually morphed into me checking his pulse.

"He called me his hero. I mean, he was kind of out of it from the bleeding and the bone setting, and he threw up again in the exam room. But saying that doesn't come from nowhere, right?"

I actually didn't know if a state of physical shock could conjure romantic pronouncements out of thin air. I had seen a lot of episodes of *House,* and with the absolutely bananas malfunctions our bodies and minds can have, it didn't seem out of the realm of possibilities. But I didn't have a definite answer and only a monster armed with educated guesses would do anything to mess up the brilliant smile on my cousin's face.

"Right, C. It's got to come from somewhere."

---

## BEN, SURGEON TO THE STARS

Ben loves the color orange because it makes him feel warm, like he is inside the sun, but totally safe. It also makes him feel alive, as does his major creative pursuit since childhood — running within the maze-like patterns of the many different rugs he has been presented with over the course of his life. As a young boy, Ben was both witness to and perpetrator of a relatively minor, yet shockingly bloody bowling accident. While his mother feared the incident might prove traumatic, Ben found the experience inspirational. It led him toward a third love, which eventually pushed past the color orange and stylized running — orthopedic surgery. Graduating top of his class, he formed a small practice in midtown Manhattan, where many of his patients are top Broadway stars. His life seemed to come full circle when he saw a man sitting on his exam table complaining of an adolescent hand injury that had always ached if he held his jazz hands for too long. When Ben offered to perform the surgery pro bono, he wasn't sure if it was a gesture of apology or of thanks.

# CHAPTER EIGHT

**Life is never fair, and perhaps it is a good thing for most of us that it is not.**

−OSCAR WILDE

I must have looked like I was waiting for a date. A date I had put way too much pressure on, pressure that was threatening to burst out unless I kept in constant motion. My left leg was bouncing up and down at a dangerous rate, and my fingers were not so much drumming against the table as savagely beating it, like I was killing bugs that didn't just scare me but had somehow wronged me. I picked up my phone, checking for new texts, messages that I imagined would say things like *Sorry, not really interested in meeting a long-lost niece after all.* After some back and forth with Sandra, but no actual messages exchanged with her mom, Emily, I was sitting at a coffee shop waiting for a meeting that could be completely life changing—you know, no pressure.

I glanced at my phone to see a text from Algie that said, "Remember to ask about familial diseases — knowledge is power." I smiled, but it felt a little off, and I instinctually looked down. Algie had informed me that when I'm super stressed and try to smile, I tend to look like someone who hasn't slept in a week. Which was why I was staring at the table when I heard my name being called, as a question. I looked up.

The woman in front of me had my eyes. I had read that phrase a million times, openly mocked the trope in books, puzzled over fictional characters and real-life people on the *Today* show getting weepy when their blood bond suddenly manifested, according to them, in the form of two eyes they were very familiar with on another person. I didn't get it then. I got it now. It was like proof I came from somewhere — that in a world that sometimes seemed like a giant jumble of people, there was a line I could hold on to.

"It's nice to meet you, Janey. I'm Emily. It's really, really nice to meet you," she said, sitting down. I sort of loved that she didn't ask for confirmation. Once I looked up, she knew. She must have seen her eyes, too.

"Thanks for meeting me," I got out in an unintentional whisper. I tried to take in little details without staring too long. My aunt (my aunt!) had short brown hair with a bright pink stripe in the front. She was wearing a light blue button-down shirt and a little silver necklace with a pendant I couldn't quite make out the shape of. She didn't seem stressed or frazzled at all. She didn't have a purse, but she did put a library book she had been carrying on the table.

"Book club," she explained, gesturing toward the paperback. I guessed my nonstaring staring tactics weren't entirely successful. "I never read it in school. Did you?"

She flipped it over and revealed the picture of the scared-looking red, white, and blue girl that had hung on Algie's wall since elementary school.

"I've seen the play. Er, the musical," I said, cursing myself for stumbling over Theater 101. I tried to think of a safe segue to the show, like how Algie and I used to perform selections from it for our parents maybe. I didn't want to explain my entire history with *Les Mis*. Like when Algie had told me, sometime after making me sit through the entire PBS special, that I was just like Cosette and that my dad was the Jean Val Jean who rescued me, which also meant that I would find true love under wonderfully dangerous and dramatic circumstances. I had cried that night, because I had never before considered that if my birth mother had given me up so I could have a better life, hers might've gotten dramatically worse and she might have had to face it alone.

"I'm really happy to meet you, Janey. I know I said that already. You know, it was Sandra's idea to do that ancestry thing. I had told her I wasn't interested in finding any biological relatives," she said.

"It was my best friend's idea. He stole my spit. For the kit, not just, like randomly. And not by force or anything, just off my straw, I think. He's not that weird. He's kind of weird. But nice. Sometimes," I rambled.

Let's clock it: four minutes into the most important meeting of my life, and I had already gone full babble. It was almost impressive. Thankfully, miraculously, she smiled in the face of my rambles.

"Sometimes you need a little push from the people who love you, right?"

"Why didn't you want to meet your relatives? Your bio relatives, I mean? Sandra said you once tried to find your birth parents . . ." I trailed off as I watched her expression cloud over. I had wrecked the moment with my directness, which isn't even a trait I could claim so much as a symptom of overloaded nerves. She shook off the shadow with a little tilt of her head and focused on my face, considering me. I hadn't really been considered often, or if I had, I hadn't noticed. I wondered what she saw, besides our eerily similar eyes. Was red lipstick the right choice, or did I go too bold?

"Are you— I know this is an oddly personal question, but your family—your parents—do you get along?" she asked.

"Yes. I mean, sometimes we fight. Because, you know, rebellion is an important part of the adolescent life-stage, or at least that's what our health teacher told us. But my parents are kind of the best," I said, and smiled. It's a dorky truth to tell, but also an easy one.

"My parents are the best, too. The people who adopted me, I mean. And growing up, I barely thought about the two other people. It was like thinking about God, I guess. I knew someone was responsible for my being, my existence, but did that really matter in the face of the two people who were responsible for making me *me?*"

I nodded. I wasn't fully onboard with the whole God metaphor since I went back and forth on their existence whereas I was one hundred percent certain some man and woman out there were responsible for whipping up my genetic makeup. But I knew what she meant. She took a little breath before going on, not overly dramatic, but noticeable. It was the kind of rev up that comes in front of a story you haven't told a lot, but you've thought about a lot.

"When I was in my early twenties, I got a little more curious. I was married, starting to imagine a life with children—that's the narrative I think of, but honestly it could have just as easily been triggered by some kind of adoption-themed movie I caught the trailer for. It was the early '90s, and there seemed to be more and more adoptees with technically closed adoptions making a few phone calls, doing just a little digging, and finding that, of course, most things that have been closed by people can be opened again. So, I tried. I contacted the agency, they refused to give me any information. I tried to look into the hospital records. I went to the library, and I just started looking through the card catalog, wracking my brain for a question I could possibly ask the librarian. 'Excuse me, do you have a copy of *Tracking Down Your Birth Parents for Dummies?*' So eventually I just, I did the craziest thing I could do. I put up a notice online."

"Online, like . . ." I started, not wanting to insult her, but needing an explanation of what exactly existed online a full decade before my birth. I was pretty sure that until the early 2000s, the internet was just a wasteland of pixelated primordial GIFs and that brain-breaking dial-up noise '90s kids seem to like so much.

"There wasn't social media, of course. But there were message boards. People were so excited to be understood by people across the country, across the world — people who were just as obsessed with *The X-Files* as they were or spent their days alone at home because they were too afraid to step outside, or people who had given up their children decades ago and never imagined something like this would be invented that might help find them. So, I posted my information on an adoptee/birth-family board. The hospital where I was born, the date, actually helpful stuff, and stuff I imagined might be helpful. A birthmark on my knee I thought my birth mother might have noticed before handing me over, a kiwi allergy I thought might be familial —"

"It is," I said, not caring for a minute about the rudeness of interrupting. "I have a kiwi allergy. So it does run in . . . our family."

She smiled, and I smiled back, relaxing fully for just a moment.

"Well, maybe including that detail wasn't as silly as I always thought it was. Anyhow. I posted it, and I'd come back to my computer every night after work, praying for a little message icon. I'm grateful, looking back, that it was before smart phones, because I'm sure I would have driven into a tree checking obsessively. And a whole month went by. And then . . . I got a message. She was there, real, writing to me. Her name was Janice. She had been looking for me, too. I guess she knew that was the right thing to say. Even if you aren't curious yourself, you always hope, deep down, that you're being looked for, right?" she asked, fiddling with her coffee cup.

I shrugged and looked down. I wanted to agree with her. Part of me did. But there had also been so many nights in second grade (when my parents started to worry kids might mention the Bag Baby thing and decided to preempt them by explaining my origin story in as much detail as you could give to a seven-year-old) that I spent imagining my birth family was searching for me. And I was so, so scared they would find me and take me away from my parents. It was that fear, I was kind of starting to realize now, that was the biggest reason I hadn't looked before now.

"Anyway, we agreed to meet. At a Starbucks, the first one they built downtown. I've never obsessed about my outfit so much, about what I should do with my hair, how much makeup I should wear. I didn't tell anyone. I know why I didn't tell my parents. I was terrified to have that conversation with them, to hurt them, to have them maybe think I thought they weren't enough. It looks so stupid in retrospect to meet with a stranger and not tell anyone, even in a public place. But I think, now, it was my way of showing her absolute trust. That there was no way she was anyone but my mother, who had been searching for me, who loved me, who would never do me any harm."

Emily stopped, and I realized I was holding my breath, waiting for what I knew wouldn't be a beautiful conclusion, but I also didn't know exactly how devastating it would be. Had this woman actually, physically hurt her? For a brief flash I had a true-crime panic moment, brought on by Algie's podcasts and all the Flannery O'Connor I'd read last semester. What if Emily brought her last thought to a dramatic twist, whispering under her breath, as she plunged the knife she had tucked between the pages of *Les Mis* into my side, "Did you think I would do you harm?"

"You okay, Jane?" she asked, looking concerned and not at all homicidal. I nodded and made the uncharacteristically smart choice not to elaborate.

"I know Sandra told you it was a scam. Janice, first of all, looked to be about two years older than me. And I think she was actually quite a bit younger than that. She had overestimated, I think, how much the drugs had aged her. I remember sitting at home weeks later thinking about her, almost overcome with pity, when I realized that she looked in the mirror and saw someone so distant from who she was, she believed she could pass for a woman in her forties."

"Did she, I mean, did she try to convince you, or . . ." I trailed off.

"No. I think she saw it in my face the moment she sat down that it wasn't going to work. I started to get up before she took off her coat.

She mumbled something. I don't know if it was an apology, or to ask for something. I wasn't really in a state of mind for either. So I just left."

"And that was enough to convince you . . . not to try again?" I asked.

I winced a little at how accusatory that sounded, like she was a quitter because she didn't want to deal with another emotional blow. But she just smiled again. I was so relieved that she seemed to find my endless conversational missteps charming.

"No. I think I would have tried again. I'm not easily discouraged. But when I got home and listened to my answering machine — You've heard of answering machines? Magical devices that people left messages on that could only be accessed when a person was home? Maybe you've seen them in the talking pictures?"

She smiled, and I smiled back, happy to learn she could be just as corny as my dad and just as certain that anyone born after 1990 had never seen a movie set before 2019.

"So you interacted with this strange device, and . . ." I said, leading.

"My mother had called. My father had had a heart attack. He was okay. He was fine, it was pretty minor. But she had been calling and calling and she was scared and had been alone in the ER waiting room because I was meeting up with some stranger. And I know now, I knew even then, that the universe wasn't punishing me for trying to find my birth family. I knew it wasn't some kind of either/or situation. The blue pill or the red pill. Do they teach classic cinema at your school?"

"Yes, I've seen *The Matrix*," I said.

"Glad to hear it. But. My epiphany. Or maybe that's too dramatic a label. No, it's accurate. It was a clarifying moment. I promise I'm not into crystals or anything, and I have no patience for meditation — don't tell Sandra — but I can't think of a better way to describe it. It clarified things. I didn't need to keep looking. I have my family. And I don't fault anyone for trying. I don't want you to think that I'm judging people who try. But I just couldn't spend any more time or energy on it. I just left it up to the universe. If fate wants to drop some family in my lap, I said to the universe, that would be fine. I swear, I'm not as much of a hippie as I sound like right now," she said.

"It's okay. I like hippies. Plus, the universe must have been listening because, you know, here I am. Dropped into your lap. Metaphorically." I laughed, and she joined in, not because it was a particularly good joke, but because I think we both felt like the big moment had been taken care of. At least for her, I mean. Her story had been told. And I had listened. I was still there, smiling. Laughing, even.

"But what about you, Janey. What are you looking for?" she asked. I waited for her to clarify, to narrow the question down. But she didn't. She just looked at me expectantly. Expecting me to tackle a college application–level question lobbed at me from the first blood relative I had ever met. I really wished I had gotten a cup of tea, if only to have something to do with my hands.

"I honestly don't know. I'm looking for . . . proof that I come from somewhere . . . good?" I said. I didn't realize how true it was until I said it out loud. My biggest question of all. I had grown up with such good people taking such good care of me, while picturing so many terrible things about the people who had left me. More than anything else, I wanted someone to tell me, definitively, that there was something good in them, too.

Her smile was a little sad this time.

"Oh, honey. Even if you keep looking, you might not find that proof. But you are somewhere good right now?"

"I am. I'm in a good place," I said. "You're good, right?" was what I wanted to add, as incredibly childish as it sounded. Some genetic good. I pictured that moment in *Spider-Man* when his DNA fractures and is replaced with radioactive spider genes, pulsing and red. I wanted a little heart or rainbow or any other pleasant Lucky Charms marshmallow in my DNA. Metaphorically. But I didn't say any of that.

My aunt smiled, then slid over a crinkly brown bag that contained an oversize frosted cookie shaped like a flower. I thanked her and took a bite. My aunt had bought me a cookie.

"So, I didn't want to spring any more relations on you than you were ready for, but Sandra's actually shopping around here, and she'd love to meet you, if that's something you're up for? Absolutely no pressure," she said.

"Of course! I'd love to meet her. And ask her what exactly salt caves are."

Emily laughed and picked up her phone, shooting off a quick text.

"I feel like we went right to the big stuff and skipped some very important small talk. Sandra said you're a senior, right?"

"Yeah, graduation is about a month away—"

I didn't get a chance to finish my thought, because I was very suddenly being hugged by Sandra, who had materialized next to our table.

"Janey! It's great to meet you. So you've met mom, great. I assume you've done the whole adopted-kid bonding thing, feelings have been shared — always glad to swoop in right after the catharsis," she said, letting me go and pulling up a chair, then sitting on it backwards and resting her arms on the top, a move that showed such complete ease of being in the world that I was immediately impressed.

"Mom and I know what's going on with us, but what's going on with you? Senior year, right? I remember. What do you have on the end-of–high school agenda? Are you going to be prom queen? In charge of the big senior prank? Leading the soccer team to victory?" Sandra asked. I wondered if she had that kind of incredible senior year herself or if she was basing her idea of what #SeniorLife was like on teen movies. The whole time she grilled me, she was also texting with one hand and trying to jam her straw through the plastic over her bubble tea with the other. I watched as her mom took the straw from her and jammed it through. She gave Emily a fist bump. It made me wish my mom was there, though that would have involved telling my parents about the whole bio family thing — a conversation I definitely wasn't ready to have.

"Uh, not shooting for prom queen, but I am going to prom," I said.

"Awesome. With friends? With a date? With a celebrity? Honestly, I don't get jealous of you youths a lot, but asking celebrities to dances was so not an option when I was in high school."

"Oh, well, probably with friends, except, well, my friends are going as a couple, so I guess that could get awkward . . ."

I hadn't really let myself picture what prom would be for me as the third wheel for Algie and Cecil, but now I could see the three of us posing by the staircase and my stomach clenched. Maybe I should ask Raina if she wanted to go as friends?

"There's no one you might want to bring?" Sandra asked, wiggling her eyebrows at me. Sandra was obviously a lot, but I was used to people being a lot. I was actually used to loving people who were a lot.

"Well, I mean, there is a girl I've been kind of seeing . . ."

I held my breath for a second to see if there'd be any reaction and let it out when I saw that neither of them looked remotely rattled by my mini–coming out.

"And . . . why isn't she your prom date?" Sandra probed.

That . . . was an excellent question, with a lot of potential answers. Because she was going with someone else to her prom. Because asking her now, after Algie had already tried to ask her for me, seemed humiliating. Because things were going so wonderfully and asking her to prom would be such a big deal that I'd run the risk of finally scaring her off.

"It's complicated" is what I went with.

"Are you nervous about living up to the promposals?" Sandra asked.

Before I could say anything, she turned to Emily and explained.

"High schoolers are doing these elaborate proposals to ask people to prom now, with cupcakes and sometimes puppies and, way too often, crime."

She turned back to me.

"I run all the social media accounts for the caves, so I try my best to keep up with youth culture."

It sounded like she was more up on it than I was. I'd seen a few cupcake- and balloon-filled promposals, but I had definitely missed the ones with crime. I wondered what kind of illegal activity could possibly convince someone to accept a prom invitation.

"I hadn't really thought about doing a promposal. I mean, we aren't even officially dating, so it might be too soon—"

"Janey, I know it might be a little too early in our relationship for me to impart some cousinly advice"—that definitely wasn't a thing— "but it's what I wish someone had told me when I was in high school. Barring criminal activity and the consequences of unprotected sex" —Emily let out a little groan and shook her head—"this is one of the last times in your life you'll be given a clean slate. Every embarrassing thing, social faux pas, beef with your teacher or seatmate simmering right under the surface, will completely disappear the minute you graduate. I personally believe every moment in your life is a moment to be bold, although I recognize that's a personal decision. But if there's a time in life when everyone should be bold, you're in it."

Sandra smiled at me, and then took a big sip of her bubble tea. Emily gave her a weary-looking smile and turned back to me.

"My daughter has always wanted to be Dear Abby, Janey. But I do think in this case she has a point. Would you like to go to the prom with this girl?"

*Like* wasn't nearly a strong enough word for how I felt when I allowed myself to daydream about Gwen as my prom date. Even though the movies had been amazing, along with the kiss at the bowling alley, what I pictured as the pinnacle of romance was a slow dance with a disco ball covering us in bits of shimmery light, my head on Gwen's shoulder as we held each other tightly, but not desperately. You don't need to keep a desperate hold on someone when you're so sure that this is just the first slow dance in a very, very long playlist.

I nodded.

"So," Sandra said, pulling a notebook and a handful of pens in different colors out of her purse. "We need a plan of action. There are the practical concerns, of course: the where, the support team, and the personalization — you know, what kind of puppies would she best respond to . . . Oh! Timeline! When is your prom?"

"One month away," I half whispered, staring as she pulled out a bottle of Wite-Out and a three-color highlighter.

"Okay, so we're officially in crunch time. Which is actually my favorite time," Sandra said, scribbling something in her notebook.

———

## SANDRA SNOOT, PROFESSIONAL AMATEUR CHEERLEADER

Born on what she insists on describing as the cusp of the cusp of Sagittarius (which, yes, is technically Scorpio), Sandra spent her formational years as a competitive cheerleader. Though she was proud of her backhand springs (and very sorry about all the damage they had on her parents' drywall), she began to get frustrated that her cheering wasn't really directed at anyone but the judges — and they seemed confident enough.

With the help of a few friends, she was able to organize North Jersey High's Need a Little Cheering program. Anyone from theater kids prepping for an audition to lovestruck youth psyching themselves up to ask their crush out was able to sign up and ride along to cheer competitions. Sitting in the stands, they would know that the entire North Jersey squad was tumbling, jackknifing, and cartwheeling just for them.

Post-graduation, Sandra took the spirit of her cheerleading days with her to college (she bought finals-care package boxes in bulk) and her first job (never have mindfulness-spa employees gotten so many literal gold stars).

While she acknowledges the potential for future issues, she is very proud of the fact at least ten different people have her listed as their emergency contact. As she explains, "They know I'd come fast and I'd come with at least two bags of chocolate."

# CHAPTER NINE

Every woman is a rebel, and usually in wild revolt
against herself.

−OSCAR WILDE, *A WOMAN OF NO IMPORTANCE*

The promposal is a delicate art, something that must be considered carefully. *It cannot be rushed* is what I wrote underneath the heading "Best Proposal Idea/Plan" once I was back home in my room, ready to maybe think about putting Sandra's suggestions into action. I knew I was really dragging my feet on this because of the lack of contractions in my description. There's just so much that can go wrong with a dramatic gesture. The line between the story you tell your grandchildren and the story you tell the cops can be thin. I had to show Gwen that I was creative, and thoughtful, without letting her know exactly what percentage of my creative, thoughtful thoughts were usually about her (it was a percentage I didn't even want to examine myself). I considered calling Algie. I considered that involving Algie was all but inevitable and avoiding asking him for help was just another way of stalling. I considered forgetting this whole thing, convincing myself it was easier to die alone, and bingeing some *Buffy* instead. Before I could really weigh my options, my FaceTime icon started to bounce.

Algie and Cecil's faces filled up my computer screen. Or actually, Algie's face and like a fourth of Cecil's. Algie didn't really share a camera frame with anyone.

"How did it go?" Algie asked.

"It was good. They're good," I said, trying to keep things vague as I hadn't actually told Cecil about the whole bio cousin thing yet. "And meeting with them kind of . . . inspired me, I guess? Or does it count as inspiration if she suggested something directly?" I wondered.

"Janey, someday you're going to have to deliver an important message, and somewhere in the middle everyone is going to die because of your obsession with prolonging the inevitable. What did Sandra suggest?" Algie asked.

"I'm going to ask Gwen to prom. With a promposal."

Suddenly Algie fell out of the frame like someone just opened a trap door under his feet and Cecil's face filled the screen, beaming.

"Oh my god, Janey, this is such a good idea. She'll love it. Your whole school will go crazy. Everyone loves a public display of true love. How are you going to do it? Did you see that one where the guy used a pony?"

"Used it to do . . . what?"

"I mean, does it really matter? I'm pretty sure the girl got to keep the pony once she said yes."

Just as I was pointing out that keeping the pony seemed highly impractical, I heard Algie, his voice kind of muffled, say, "Exactly what would have become of the pony if she said no?"

"You guys are the worst, but obviously we're ignoring that at the moment because right now we're helping Janey. What do you need? I can fit in a locker," Cecil said.

"I guess if you guys want to help me think of the exact details for the whole thing, that would be nice," I sort of muttered, giving up on maintaining any semblance of dignity.

"Yes! We'll be, like, your Cyranos!" Cecil practically yelped. I'm pretty sure he was equally excited by the prospect and proud of his AP English reference.

"So, I guess I'm going to have to be the incredibly hot realist, like always, but before Cecil starts humming *Mission Impossible,* or something, I want to point out that Excelsior Academy for Incredibly Wealthy and Virtually Poreless Young Ladies is pretty much a fortress. Parents spend Ivy League tuition money to make sure their little angels are safe. So before we find out just how many people on Craigslist are willing to deliver a pony to Connecticut for a small fee, you should probably figure out how you're actually going prompose," Algie said.

I was frustrated and relieved, the two emotions warring in a way that had a strangely positive effect on my posture. Maybe this was a sign from the universe, or God, like that story Cecil's dad liked to tell about the dude in the flood who keeps praying to be saved, and ignores the rowboats and Coast Guard because he wants God himself to pick him up. And if I didn't see this hitch in the plan — of the near impossibility of getting into Gwen's school — as a sign this entire plan was doomed, then an all-powerful deity would be up there watching, cringing.

"She doesn't need to do it at Gwen's school," Cecil shouted suddenly, like this was the most obvious solution in the world.

"But that's where you have promposals," I pointed out.

"That's where unimaginative people have promposals. You could have yours in Central Park," Cecil said, with a triumphant look on his face.

"Central Park," I repeated. I know it's this big famous place, this green oasis in an urban sprawl, as my middle school history teacher told us. But it's kind of hard to appreciate its bigness when you're just in one spot, and it's hard to think of it as an oasis when it smells like horse poop and there are approximately two hundred screaming children there at all times. My only notable memory from Central Park was dropping my King Cone ice cream down on an exceptionally chill pigeon that didn't even break its little jerky stride. Some kid in a stroller took in the scene, then pointed at the cone and said, "Birthday hat." It wasn't a bad memory, but it also didn't make me think of romance.

"Oh my god," Algie said.

"What?"

"It's possible I have some information obtained after a very, very wine-soaked Easter party at Gwen's house that could help," Algie said.

"And that information is . . ." I prodded.

"A certain movie snob, who I swear to god made me turn off *Shrek* when we were six years old because it was 'tacky,' might have, under a great deal of influence, confessed to me that she actually really loves *Enchanted*."

I know it's probably a little hyperbolic to say that anything is possible in New York City. But what I did know for a fact is that anything that can be achieved with a large amount of theater students is possible in New York City. Because they are everywhere, they have the stamina of people who take Monster energy drinks intravenously, and they will work all day for three boxes of Munchkins. Which was how Algie became the director of a very limited-run re-creation of the Central Park scene from the movie *Enchanted*. Algie was directing because my attempts at direction sounded very much like suggestions, and apparently suggesting stuff wasn't the most effective way to get thirty freshmen from the American Musical and Dramatic Academy to learn their choreography.

"God, Brian, what are you not getting? It's three turns clockwise, three counterclockwise!" Algie yelled at a kind of stunning aspiring film actor who had managed to bungle every single one of Algie's stage directions in a new and exciting way.

"Dude, no one has, like, circle clocks anymore," Brian said, pushing a perfectly formed wave of hair out of his eyes, which were so beautifully blue, I could almost forget he totally looked like the type of guy who'd call the #MeToo movement a slippery slope. I tried not to think about what it said about my obviously black soul that I was having a moment of lust during prep for a promposal.

"I don't have time to address that. Just look at the people to your left and right who have probably had a similar amount of 'circle-clock' interaction as you and have managed to figure this out, and follow them." Algie sighed in exasperation that he'd stopped trying to mask about twenty takes ago.

"I love it when he takes charge," Cecil said, handing me an incredibly misshapen ice cream SpongeBob on a stick before taking a bite out of his own SpongeBob.

"Then you must love him all the time."

"I think I do," Cecil sighed. I licked the vaguely lemony ice cream, trying to figure out the best response.

I put my head on Cecil's shoulder. I had given Algie such a hard time, but he was actually turning into the best boyfriend Cecil had ever had. Ever since the bowling alley, Algie had been attentive and sweet in a way I had only seen him act when I broke my leg in seventh grade and he arranged for a group of kids in his building to cart me around the city in a giant wagon. These days, Algie even texted me questions about Cecil's favorite foods and music so he could surprise him with snacks and perfect playlists.

"I really wish you had the budget for a trained squirrel. Or the kind of relationship with a nonprofessional squirrel that they'd join in for free," Raina said, appearing so suddenly by the rock we were perched on that Cecil almost toppled off.

"Raina, oh my god, hi. What are you doing here?" I asked.

"Would you believe that Algie called me in as a creative collaborator?"

Cecil and I said no in unison.

"Then you know your friend well, which I think is really beautiful. Algie mentioned the plan at play practice the other day, and I do love to watch the machinations of courtship. And experience the sense of danger that comes from a kind of collective amnesia when you enter Central Park that the mini-roads are for bikes, horse drawn carriages, and pedestrians," Raina said, punctuating her statement with a few circular swirls of the dance ribbon she pulled from inside her sleeve.

"As a more practical matter, my ribbons have broken three of my grandmother's fans this week, so I thought it might be best to use them outside the apartment for a while," she added.

Any more questions about how a ribbon dancer could take out that many fans, or why ribbon dance practice was needed, were pre-empted by Algie's bellowing. Or, directing.

"If the unfurling of the banner isn't at tempo, then this isn't a promposal, it's just an unlicensed staging of the intellectual property of the most litigious company in the country. So, let's get on beat. Kim —I see you checking your Apple Watch. He hasn't texted you, probably because he knows you have somehow managed to murder a jazz square. We have this spot for thirty more minutes before the Quidditch league takes over, so let's do this again, and let's do it on! The! Beat!" Algie practically screamed.

I watched as the women spun, fell into the arms of the men, and then the front line began to slowly unfurl the banner Algie had stolen from the theater department and Cecil had hand-lettered on the back GWEN, COME TO THE PROM WITH ME. IT WILL BE ENCHANTING. The wording was not my choice. First of all, I didn't like the fact that my ask wasn't really an ask, but a statement. A command. But Algie had reasoned that without the gendered power imbalance that could sour a command from a guy to a girl, and because Gwen was, in general, attracted to people who spoke their minds and went after what they wanted, I should consider the "ask" a forgone conclusion. Cecil had added something about manifesting what you want through the power of positive thinking, but both Algie and I chose to ignore him. The *Enchanted* pun was Cecil's suggestion, but I quickly seconded it. It wasn't terribly witty or anything, but bad wordplay is kind of part of the whole promposal tradition. Sometimes you have to honor the nervous, lovestruck teens who came before you.

"Okay. Take five. Take ten. Take however long it takes to get on the goddamn beat. Do you have your metronomes?" Algie asked, and I watched as all thirty dancers pulled out their phones and turned them to him, revealing their metronome apps clicking in a reassuringly consistent rhythm.

"Good. Now go and listen to them until the beat is under your skin, in your blood, and in your aura—just as long as it somehow migrates into your feet!" Algie shouted, turning three times, clockwise, before marching toward us.

"Hey, Raina. You've come to witness my grand creation?" Algie asked, as he sat down with us on the rock and leaned against Cecil's chest.

"I'd like to think I witness that every day, Algie," she said, spinning around the rock and moving out into the grassy area to give her ribbon dance more room. Three separate butterflies landed on her head as she continued to dance. I knew science would probably pin that on the plumes of cotton-candy perfume wafting off her and her very realistic-looking flower crown, but I was leaning toward their having whatever nonprofessional relationship she recognized we don't have with squirrels.

"I think I've found my calling. My vocation. My reason for being put on this earth that is swiftly being swallowed by the sea," Algie declared as Cecil offered him the last bite of his SpongeBob.

"I think technically the sea is part of the earth, so I don't think it can be swallowed by itself, right?" I asked, more to mess with Algie than to start a philosophical debate on the technicalities of the apocalypse.

"So, let me guess, let me guess. You're going to be a metronome craftsman. No, wait, you're going to become an educational activist, but the only thing you're going to focus on is teaching kids how to read time on a circle clock? Or you're going to become a hit man and focus exclusively on people who are off beat?" I suggested, as Cecil started giggling.

"Janey, Janey, you can't bother me today. I am at peace. I thought I would face up to a year of struggle as an aspiring actor before I'm discovered, but now I know I can bypass all that character-building strife to follow my true passion—to be a director!" Algie said, swinging his arm out like he was wielding an imaginary sword, which made me even more worried about the future people "lucky" enough to be under his direction.

"But, um, Algie? Isn't it kind of hard to make it as a director, too?" asked Cecil. "I mean, I totally know you will—like, I can picture you winning the Oscar and everything—but don't you think there might be, like, a little character-building struggle?"

"Maybe, Cecil, in the old days. But now directors don't have to wait for producers to recognize their brilliance. They just grab a camera, thirty acting students, crowd source if they have to—"

"Hit up their comically rich parents," I interjected.

"I might ask for a small loan. But they'll get it all back once I'm wildly successful," Algie said.

"Should I point out—" I started.

"The average college student changes their major four times," Algie said.

"Do they normally change it before they even go to freshman orientation?" I asked.

"Whatevs! I'm not average anyway," Algie said, tipping his head back against Cecil so he could give him an upside-down kiss.

I looked out at the crowd assembled, my soon-to-be fellow college students in black hoodies with their school logos and black beanies and Doc Martens and Converse, all in an unofficial uniform. They also seemed to be standing in a kind of uniform haze of excited panic, which I thought might be coming less from just the prospect of Algie getting back on his bullhorn in under ten minutes, and more from the general hoping and praying that they'd make it. I would never want to be an actress in a million years. The thought of going up in front of a group of strangers and saying, "Hi, I'm here for you to pass judgment on," made me feel sick. But I kind of got the feeling now. Of having so much hope next to so much fear of disappointment.

"Can we go over the plan one more time?" I asked.

Algie, whose face was tilted toward the sun, eyes closed, groaned as Cecil launched into the promposal battle plan.

"Algie is going to text Gwen to meet him in Central Park to help with some kind of leaf collecting project, which she'll totally buy as something a last-semester senior would be assigned because she has no idea what actually happens in public school. You will be with Algie, and with very little effort — because as I keep trying to tell you, Janey, Gwen's so obviously into you — you'll suggest you take a walk around the fountain, at which point the flash mob will flash, the banner will unfurl, she'll say yes, and the two of you will make out in front of all of the tourists," Cecil finished, smiling.

"You guys realize there's, like, three weeks until prom, and with all our time and effort going into Janey's spectacle, we haven't sorted out anything else. Are we taking a limo? A party bus? What are our after-party options? We need to order the flowers or we'll end up stuffing bodega daisies into my tux. And I know I can pull anything off, but that doesn't mean I want to be forced to pull that off," Algie said.

And then Cecil was showing us his phone, the screen full of a gorgeous deep purple rose.

"I already ordered it for you. I just remember, like, this fact that's been stuck in my head since fourth grade that purple was for royalty, and I think, with your suit, you'll look kind of regal. I mean, not that you don't without a suit; I mean with different, everyday clothes." Algie cut Cecil off with a kiss, and when I realized it was less a kiss and more of a starting gun for what looked like a dangerously intense make-out session to be having on the edge of a sharp rock, I hopped off and started to walk by the baseball diamond. I loved the sound of the ball hitting the metal bat. I assume there's some reason the professional teams use wood, maybe something about physics or tradition, but I think they're crazy for not filling their stadiums with that satisfying clink. This detail made its way into my wildest fantasies about Gwen and me. Fantasies beyond prom and slow dancing with my head on her shoulder and lacing our fingers together in front of her mother and random people on the subway. I envisioned a future when she'd know I like the sound of a ball hitting a metal bat — a future when she'd hear it and think of me and smile, and rush home to tell me that she was thinking about me that day.

## ALGERNON MONCRIEFF, CONTINUES TO LIVE (IS A VAST UNDERSTATEMENT)

Algernon Moncrieff was born to Raquel and Edward Moncrieff on the same day *Kangaroo Jack* was released in theaters. It was a fact that would haunt him until the day he died (he predicted). Algernon spent most of his youth attending theater camps across New York, dazzling his peers with his talents in acting and getting takeout delivered to whatever corner of the woods they were performing *Into the Woods* in.

When he's not honing his craft, he's often at the YMCA teaching the tiniest thespians the importance of diction and not picking your nose (at least not during the climatic moments). He will continue to survive with his best friend, Jane Worthing; his camp rival and reigning frenemy, Jason Michelson; his cousin Gwendolyn Fairfax; and many others, who will detail their relationship with him in their own words.

Though sometimes clinically pessimistic, Algernon does believe, if not in the power of love, then in the power of spectacle. His love of theater and love for experiencing theater with others led him to create a series of "take a ticket" spots across New York City. The deli-style machines dispense Broadway tickets and are hidden in massive and ever-changing scavenger hunts (though Algernon will often give hints to senior citizen and student centers across Manhattan). Algernon is known for his favorite catch phrase, dramatically called out after every curtain call, which his friends know is one of the most earnest sentiments he has ever shared — "I'm so glad you could come."

Please continue to send flowers on opening nights. Algie loves them.

# CHAPTER TEN

**Friendship is far more tragic than love. It lasts longer.**

–OSCAR WILDE

Prom was in fourteen days, and I lacked a dress, a date, and the energy to do much about getting either. Stress had eaten away at my immune system and left me in a heap of used tissues and shriveled Capri-Sun pouches. I had to postpone meeting up with Sandra, which also pushed back me telling my parents I was in contact with blood relatives. Luckily, being suddenly diseased meant I had little brainpower to tackle either issue. Or the two branches of the same issue. Or the ability to create coherent metaphors about my issues.

I felt my phone buzz and looked down to see two texts, one from Sandra and one from Emily. Emily had been texting me fairly regularly since we met up, almost exclusively links to local news reports of promposals with notes tacked on like—"This seems sweet" and "I know you have it all figured out, but thought this could help!" Her decision to keep all conversations to one safe subject made me like her more, seeing as it was apparently a familial coping mechanism. I had once talked to a friend at dance class about nothing but the solar system for a full year.

Sandra's texts were more varied—the latest a link to a recipe for healing ginger tea then a collection of GIFs depicting different animals as doctors, followed by another reminder that as soon as I was less dead, I had to come with her to the salt caves.

Lying in bed under a pile of blankets, at first I was too distracted by the questions a giraffe with a stethoscope triggered to notice Algie's appearance. It then took multiple attempts to pitifully raise my head a few inches off my sick bed to see Algie, or who I assumed was Algie, standing in my doorway holding a can of Lysol. It was hard to be one hundred percent sure it was him, though, as he was dressed in a complete replica plague-doctor outfit, black robe, beak mask, and all.

"Hold on, I need to take a picture for the next time you insist you're not a drama queen," I rasped, pawing at my sheets for my phone before giving up with a sigh and pausing the movie playing on my laptop.

"It's dramatic to think of my health? I'm a shining beacon of responsibility. Speaking of shining, the whole fever sheen is giving your face the kind of dimension you've never achieved with a highlighter. I'd snap a few selfies before it breaks," he said, the mask muffling his voice.

"I'm sorry, I'm not really up for a photoshoot right now. You see, I'm dying. I wasn't sure about it before, but then a literal harbinger of death showed up at my doorstep, so —"

"Now who's being dramatic? A+ for the SAT word even when you're working with . . . what, 101 degrees?"

"102."

"Respectable," he said, letting off a cloud of disinfectant. Algie was the only person I knew whose competitive streak extended to all-time fever highs. (His record: 104, pneumonia on a family ski trip last winter. He dated the candy striper at the local hospital all spring).

"So why have you risked coming to the hot zone?" I asked, before dissolving into a coughing fit.

"To remind you to drink your orange juice, generally lift your spirits, and make sure you're prepared to be a part of my masterpiece."

"Your masterpiece. You mean my promposal?"

"It might be your story, Janey, but it's my vision. My direction is what will make your longing, your feelings of love, truly come to life."

"Good. Great. I've been stressing, and now I know you've got the whole thing handled. Actually, it kind of sounds like I don't even need to be there. You ask Gwen for me, okay? If I'm not already dead. But I probably will be. From Gila monster flu."

"There's no such things as Gila monster flu."

"There is now. I'm patient zero. Don't let Gwen come visit me, no matter how she begs. It's too dangerous!"

"Janey, I feel like we're swapping roles here and it's concerning. Two drama queens in one room leads to nothing but death and destruction. That's how Mary, Queen of Scots, lost her head."

"Aha! I knew you watched the movie without me. You promised we'd critique the costumes together," I said, flinging myself back onto the pillow dramatically, which turned out to be a mistake, because the room swirled violently until I closed my eyes.

"Jesus, Janey, Sephora can do nothing to help you now. You have reached a new shade of white no concealer comes in," Algie said.

I managed to crack one eye open and saw him sitting cross-legged on the floor, his head cocked to the side in the closest thing he could get to an empathetic expression with the mask on.

"It's possible that the assault on my white blood cells has brought certain anxieties to the surface," I rasped, closing my eyes again.

"Well, that's terrifying. You should always keep your anxieties deep, deep underground. Like, underneath your repressed memories. What anxieties, exactly?" Algie asked.

"You know, the general pre-grad stuff. Should I have decided to leave home instead of go to a city school next year? Will my parents feel abandoned when I tell them about Sandra and Emily, will Sandra and Emily actually abandon me, will Gwen laugh in my face at the promposal—"

"Will you abandon me as soon as you find friends who are technically 'nice'—"

"What?" I asked, jerking up so quickly the room shifted again and I had to fight the urge to black out.

"Oh, right, sorry, that one's mine. But this isn't about me. It's rude to make it about yourself at someone else's death bed, right?" His weak attempt at a laugh echoed through the plastic beak.

"Algernon Moncrieff, what are you talking about? *Best Friends Forever* is I'm pretty sure what you wrote in that way-overpriced *Book of Shadows* during your witchcraft phase, and is what our many, many Claire's key chains say, and is what you almost convinced me to get actually tattooed onto my body when you were dating that really sketchy art student you promised knew what he was doing."

"Brent did know what he was doing. His work was absolutely gorgeous. His clients just sometimes got tetanus. And if BFF key chains were some kind of binding contract, there'd be no reason for high school reunions. People lose touch. People actively seek out people who maybe fit them better, but who didn't happen to live in their school zone," he said.

"Neither of us are even leaving the city," I said. "We won't even have to change coffee shops. I think our friendship can survive different English classes."

"Then you have more faith in it at the moment than I do."

I didn't know what to say. The idea that I could lose touch with Algie, that either of us could loosen the vice grip we had on each other's lives, was completely crazy. He'd lose his last semblance of a moral compass, I'd lose the person who made sure I left the comforting glow of my laptop every so often, and we'd both lose the person who we could talk to across a crowded classroom using only steady eye contact. We didn't even really need eyebrow quirking at this point, we were beyond that.

"Didn't you wonder why I did the whole spit-heist thing?"

"A general lack of boundaries? The desperate need to be called to be a guest on a podcast? Basic boredom?" I suggested. My wondering dance card had been completely full, and it never occurred to me to make space to ask questions about something that seemed so on-brand for Algie.

"I thought," he started, first pulling off his mask, revealing a slightly sweaty face that was nowhere near the disaster it should be given the plastic sauna. "I thought if we only had time for one last adventure together, I wanted to make sure it was more memorable than a road trip upstate or an awkward double date. I wanted to make sure that even if you stopped texting me by spring break next year, at least I'd be an important figure in one story you told your new college friends. And all your friends after that."

Algie stared at his shoes, which really freaked me out. Algie doesn't look at his shoes, he makes total unnerving eye contact. I knew we should probably have a discussion about this insecurity that to me, seemed to come out of nowhere. And the fact that he was able to hide it from me is probably another conversation we'd need to have, but I didn't know how to tackle his uncertainty about something I was so certain about with words alone. Which meant I had to go with actionable steps.

"What would ease your mind, Algie? Do you want to become blood siblings? Because my blood is full of Gila monster germs at the moment, but really what solidifies a friendship more than sharing fever dreams together?" I asked, sticking out my arm like I was ready for a safety-pin prick.

"I will pass on the solidarity through snot, thanks. But there is something that could make me feel a little better," Algie said. "You know those super creepy pacts the best friends make in some of the old rom-coms your mom had us watch, the ones involving getting married at a certain age that don't only reek of heteronormativity, but seem to imply a life isn't truly a meaningful life unless you've bound yourself to someone sexually and legally until the end of time?" he asked.

"Too many words, Algie. Head, so hot. But sure, go on."

"What if we make a pact that even if we are, especially if we're all married or partnered or whatever by the time we're thirty, we'll buy a pair of rocking chairs?"

"I think I've hit the delirium phase. Rocking chairs?"

"You know, that we'll put out on the front porch and rock and people watch in when we're old. That will be our promise, to be two old friends together."

"You said you want to live in New York forever."

"So?"

"New York doesn't have porches, it has stoops."

"Some houses probably have porches. Houses in your neighborhood have porches."

"Not in Manhattan."

"Well, you can't have a rocking chair on a stoop."

"That's what I'm saying. But they're just metaphorical, right? Can we get, like, mini ones?"

"They're not metaphorical, they're incredibly literal, and they need to be big enough for us to rock in!"

"But small enough to fit on a stoop."

I watched Algie pull his mask back down, huffing in frustration and fogging up the clear plastic eye panels.

"Okay, okay, okay. Algie, I'll make you a promise. Sometime before we turn thirty, I'll figure out the logistics of becoming two old friends rocking on a New York City porch that currently doesn't exist. Does that work?" I asked.

"Yeah, that should be okay," he conceded, just as I heard footsteps in the hall.

"Hey, JJ!" Dad shouted as he walked into my room, pausing briefly to consider Algie before shrugging and holding up a Seamless bag.

"You ordered food, honey? You know, I could make you a veggie shake that would knock that bug right out of yeh!" he said, putting the bag at the foot of my bed.

"I actually, uh, didn't order anything, Dad. Maybe we got the Murphys' by mistake?"

I pulled my sheets toward me, bringing the bag closer and closer without actually having to go through the hassle of sitting up to retrieve it. Stapled to the front was the receipt from a soup place I didn't recognize. And there, underneath the name that was definitely my name and the address that was definitely my address was a message, "Get well soon. — Gwen."

I suddenly realized Dad had edged in and was reading over my shoulder.

"Wow, JJ. I had some secret admirers in my day, but no one ever sent me soup. Sounds serious. Algernon, tell it to me straight. Should I be rooting for Gwen? Is she good enough for our JJ?"

"Well, Mr. Worthing, I think that's for Janey to decide, isn't it?" Algie said in his best all-American boy voice.

"You are right, Algernon. Janey can make her own decisions. I'm going to make you a veggie shake anyway, honey. You still look pretty sick."

"And if you make me drink your sludge, Dad, I'll feel pretty sick too."

"All right, wise guy. You want a Fudgesicle?"

"Yes, please."

"Algernon, I'd offer you one, but I—"

"That's okay, Mr. Worthing. I'm going to head out anyway," Algie explained, getting up as Dad left to retrieve the Fudgesicle.

"You need to tell your parents," Algie said, stepping cautiously toward my bed. This was possibly the first time I had ever heard Algie come to that conclusion. Algie believed wholeheartedly that the best relationship you can have with your parents is built on a mutual respect for your respective lies.

"About . . ." I said, even though I knew exactly what he was talking about.

"You promise we'll get the chairs?"

"God, Algie, so needy. We are getting the chairs. You will never be rid of me. Our friendship is eternal."

"Like Twinkies," we muttered in unison. He stuck out a gloved hand in a fist, and I obliged by bumping it gently with my own.

"You fixed things for me, just now. I don't know how to do that for you, with the whole bio family thing. I'm tagging your parents in."

I raised an eyebrow at his sports reference.

"You don't hook up with as many jocks as I have and not pick up something, and, yes, I heard that and so I'm going," he said, dramatically turning and pulling his cape over his face like the Phantom of the Opera.

"See you later, Algernon," Dad called after him as he passed him in the doorway. He held a Fudgesicle in one hand and was trailed by my mother. He handed it over as they both sat on the bed. Nobody said anything for a second, a completely comfortable silence enveloping us as I slurped and tried to ignore Algie's voice in my head.

My parents wouldn't care. They'd be happy for me to make connections with bio relatives — connections that totally weren't a big deal, because who knew how long they'd last! So there was really no reason to mention anything.

I finished my pop and lay back down. My mom put her hand on my forehead, and I could feel the cold metal of her wedding ring cut through the fevered heat coming off me in waves.

"How are you feeling?" she asked.

And then I started to cry. I hadn't meant to, but the simple question broke a carefully constructed wall inside me that revealed I was feeling pretty awful. Not even Gwen and everything she made me feel could totally distract me from a question I could no longer ignore.

"Why haven't they tried to find me?"

I sobbed into my mother's shirt, a soft gray cotton one almost as old as me. My father wrapped us both in a hug, saying over the sound of my crying, "JJ sandwich." We stayed like that for a few minutes, my parents waiting until I was ready to start talking before asking questions. I finally got my breathing under control and looked up at my mother. I had always wished I had eyes that looked like hers, cool gray, but somehow full of color at the edges.

I was almost too tired to be horrified that I had finally, finally let the question slip. Or by the fact that I was going to have to explain to my parents why this question was so close to the surface of my fevered brain. Illness, or maybe just exhaustion, is an understood truth serum in the way alcohol is. I was going to have to tell them I went looking for parents who weren't them. Like someone skeezily trolling on a dating app when their lovely, loving partner is right in the other room.

"I have to tell you something," I said, propping myself up on my pillow. They looked at me expectantly.

"Algie stole my spit and then there was an acorn that proved I have a bio cousin and a bio aunt and I met them at a coffee shop downtown and for a second I did think she might be a serial killer but she's actually an insurance agent and I'm sorry I didn't tell you before."

Talking without taking a breath might be my most natural conversational style, but the lack of air winded me a little, and I slid down a few inches.

"We know, JJ," Dad said quietly.

"You — how?"

"Emily emailed me before you two met. Felt it was her duty, as another parent, to let me know."

I sat stunned for a second. I wondered if this could count as a betrayal of trust, but I figured if it happened before we actually met, it was pre-relationship. Which was something, I realized, we had now. A relationship.

"Why didn't you tell us, Janey?" Mom asked.

"I didn't want you to think I needed something . . . more than you guys," I said. It felt awful to say it out loud and look at them while I said it.

Mom smiled.

"That's very sweet, honey, but the rest of your life is going to be an endless list of what you need beyond this house, and us. We know that. Don't you think we want you to know where you come from?"

"I come from here," I said. Maybe Cecil was right and I should have been journaling. It turns out acknowledging your deepest anxieties instead of letting them slowly eat a hole through the lining of your stomach can start to clarify things pretty quickly.

"You belong here. But you come from somewhere else. Maybe it was wrong of us not to talk about that more. I don't know," Mom said. It was terrifying to realize Mom wasn't sure how to handle this either. And a little reassuring.

"We want you to get to know your whole family. All the parts," Dad said.

"If you need more answers, we can hire another detective, you know. There's so much more technology than there was even a decade ago, it might be better—"

"I think . . . I think I don't need to go looking right now," I said. It wasn't that finding Emily and Sandra answered a question or filled a hole. Or they had, a little. Enough for now. Emotionally, that was where I was at, I realized. The knowledge that I would always wonder, I would always crave knowing what had happened not just on that day at the train station, but all the days before it. I had been healthy that day, with chubby baby cheeks. Someone had taken care of me. And there were going to be moments in my life when that need would burn brighter and I'd have to do some more digging, hire that detective, fill those chapters of my life story that so many other people take for granted. This wasn't an end. It was an intermission.

"My promposal is in three days," I said. If my parents were thrown by my sudden topic change, they didn't show it.

"I don't know what that is, but it sounds dangerously close to *proposal,* which is something I hope you're not planning on doing before you graduate high school. I know you haven't gone to a wedding yet, but they're really much better when the bride and groom can legally drink," Dad said.

"*Prom-posal,* Dad. Prom. As in I'm asking Gwen — you know, from the soup? — to prom. But with, like, a musical number," I explained.

"So that's what the kids these days are doing? Well, that's a relief. My all-dad newsletter this morning said you were all binge drinking pickled museum relics, but if you're just overthinking prom invitations, I know I'll sleep easier."

"I've seen a few of the videos on the *Today* show. Just promise we won't get a call from the cops after it's over," Mom said.

"I promise. Everything is legal. Well, Algie might get in trouble with the actor's union, but I don't think that's the kind of thing you can be an accessory to."

"So, is Gwen just a prom date, or should we plan a dinner to meet your new girlfriend?" Dad asked, bouncing his eyebrows up and down in a way that was too silly to even be mock suggestive.

"I mean, Gwen isn't just anybody . . ." I trailed off. I didn't want to put any more pressure on the promposal than absolutely necessary. And imagining a future in which prom led to a relationship that led to a shared studio in the Village where we adopted a Westie named Eastie was definitely going to put more pressure on it.

"Well, that expression answers that question. You're never going to be a poker player, Janey. Okay. You should get some sleep," Mom said, getting up then pulling Dad with her. He let out an exaggerated groan before leaping down into a squat then leaping back up and bounding out the door, calling over his shoulder, "I'm still going to juice you something, JJ."

I watched Mom walk over to the door, then pause in the doorway.

"Mom?"

"I feel like I should turn on your nightlight or music box or something else you haven't needed in a million years. I miss . . . I miss being able to do the little things to make you feel safe."

"You can hit the spacebar on my laptop to restart the movie, if that would make you feel better."

She smiled and walked over to tap it, the sounds of English accents filling the room as *Sense and Sensibility* resumed.

"Thanks, Mom," I whispered as she closed the door.

I lay back down. My parents were the reason I could start the search and why I could call halftime. You can look for answers and sit with questions as long as you know someone will always be there for you, no matter what you find.

## MICKEY WORTHING, PROFESSIONAL AMATEUR ATHLETE, SURPRISE FATHER

Mickey Worthing, born and raised in Boston, had planned to be a basketball/baseball/hockey player. After a series of not-entirely-unkind coaches explained in no uncertain terms that he would never possess the hand-eye coordination required for organized sports, Worthing threw his energy, and all four limbs, into the fitness industry, which in the early '90s consisted almost entirely of Tae Bo VHS tapes. At twenty-eight he walked into the Poughkeepsie train station on his way home from the Second Annual Upstate New York Cardio Conference, and he found a one-year-old girl in a large handbag. Having never given much serious thought to fatherhood before, once the baby girl was in his arms, he would never have to give it serious thought at all. Something much simpler than thinking — instinct — informed him in that moment when he first held his daughter.

After months of parenting classes and somehow reverse engineering several different brands of playhouses into some kind of plastic compound, Worthing formally adopted his daughter, and one year later, he would meet the woman who would become his wife.

A staple at 5Ks across the tri-state area, he has been approached by baffled race officials who saw splits year after year that would put Worthing first in his age bracket, only for him to slow his pace by more than half his earlier speed in the last quarter mile. Worthing explained that he knew there were other people who needed the win more. And one of his all-time favorite things to see is the look *on someone's face as they hear their name called in victory when they really needed the win.*

———†———

That I've developed a new symptom, or that maybe everything under my skin is trying to get outside of my skin, was the first thing I thought when I woke up to an intense buzzing coming from my chest, which turned out to be my phone. Maybe I needed to stop watching DemonBug movies.

I rolled over and looked down to see Gwen's name lighting up the screen that also let me know it was ten p.m. I unlocked it and attempted to say hello, but my throat did not cooperate.

"Hell-uh," I kind of hissed.

"So I guess my soup didn't work?" Gwen asked.

"No, no, I haven't had any yet, but it looks good, and that was really sweet. It probably would work. I'll try it now —"

"Janey, take a breath. How are you?"

Possible responses flew through my mind. *Better, now that I'm talking to you* — too corny. *So . . . hot* — way too advanced: you do not jump from one suggestive suggestion to flu-based dirty talk. No, no, not that.

"Gross. I feel gross. I look gross."

It was the truth. I liked telling her the simple truth.

"I'm sorry. How can I help? Let me distract you from your sudden state of disgustingness," she said, laughing.

"Do you want to watch an episode of *Rings of Saturn* together?" I suggested.

"I would love that. Which one?" she asked, just as I said, "'The Confession,' duh."

She laughed again.

"Of course. Sending you the link now. See you in the chat."

We hung up, and I dragged myself to my laptop, hobbled back to bed with it, and tented the covers over my head and it as Gwen's icon appeared in the chat and the video started playing.

The music swelled as the camera panned the cold blue dessert.

Gwen F: Do you ever wonder why they're always in tank tops and short shorts if it's supposed to be an ice planet?

JJ : All. The. Time.

"The Confession Part 2" was the exciting conclusion of a two-part episode. Layla and Roxy, coworkers in a government lab, have just discovered that what they thought was a machine to process food is actually a weapon the government has created to take out a rival manufacturing plant. They're both wracked with guilt that they could have had a hand in creating something so destructive, and they begin to plot to destroy it without alerting government forces. But none of that is really important because just as the episode ends, a beam breaks and impales Roxy, leaving her bleeding in Layla's arms. Most fans agree that it's a kind of extreme way to get them entwined, but sometimes we shippers take what we can get.

The shot zoomed in on the pair as we watched, Roxy shivering from blood loss, Layla trying to stop some of the bleeding.

"Well, this is surprising," Roxy whispered.

"It's going to be a great story, Roxy." I mouthed the words with Layla, her most famous catch phrase, delivered through tears.

"I really wish I could get to tell it," Roxy said, a trickle of blood going down from her mouth, letting you know that this is not one of your casual, "an episode in the medevac and then she's all better" kind of impalements (which happen on fantasy shows more often than you'd think).

Gwen F: Ahhh, they're doing the forehead touch.

JJ: Yes, the forehead touch. Why do shows even bother with full-on sex scenes when they can do the forehead touch?!

"You're going to tell it. This isn't the end of your story," Layla whispered fiercely.

"I'd love a way out of this, Layla, but when a ring girl gets cold, you know that's a bad sign," Roxy said, coughing violently and then kind of weakly.

JJ: Oh my god, that's exactly what I sound like.

Gwen F: I don't want to armchair diagnose you or anything, but are you sure you have the flu and not a beam?

JJ: *checks stomach* no beam.

Gwen F: Good. Because I'm not a Siloph.

JJ: I had been wondering about that.

Roxy's breathing got more and more labored.

"Roxy. Roxy! Do you trust me?"

Roxy's eyes fluttered open.

"With my life. Though that's a . . . rapidly shrinking point of measurement."

And then Layla kissed her, a soft blue glow pulsing from her face to Roxy's as the beam disappeared and the wound closed.

"Layla, you mean . . ."

"It never seemed like the right time to bring it up."

"But that must have taken . . . The pain of it, the size, you must have lost years," Roxy whispered, noting Layla's reveal that she is a Siloph, someone with healing powers that take days, weeks, or in the case of near-death injuries, years off the Siloph's life when they dole them out. "I never would have asked you to . . ."

"I know."

"I'll admit, I never quite paid attention to it at the academy. I didn't know it would feel like that. And the music . . . Is there always music?"

JJ: I looove this line.

Gwen F: Idk. Kind of corny?

JJ: But such romantic corn.

There was a close-up shot showing just Layla's face.

"There's not. That's just the music I hear whenever I look at you.

---

KELLY TANNER, *RINGS OF SATURN*
CREATOR, FAN FICTION CHAMPION

Kelly Tanner was just another teenager on FanficPlace.net in the early '90s when a chance encounter with a stranger changed her life. She was sitting at her favorite little cafe when a man at the table next to her began choking on a chocolate croissant. With her summer lifeguard training, she ran over to give him the Heimlich maneuver, saving his life. He insisted on buying her a hot chocolate in thanks, and as they began chatting, he noticed the open fic on her laptop. He was completely entranced, reading the entire chapter in one sitting. Only when he finished, tears streaming down his face, did he reveal his true identity — he was Matthew Spinnet, the executive director of Sci-Fi/Fantasy TV. He explained it must have been fate that brought them together and offered her the chance to run her own show on the spot, claiming she was the only person to break through to him emotionally with the power of narrative in over ten years.

Actually, Kelly started as a craft services worker in high school, eventually scoring the job of an assistant, working long hours on set and even longer hours working on her pilot. After over a decade in the industry, countless failed pitches, and at least seven tearful confessions to her girlfriend that she was never going to make it and that they would both be so much happier if they just bought that old bakery like they joked about, she finally signed the contract to produce the first season of *Rings of Saturn*.

But she would prefer to have you believe the first story. It would be so much more interesting to produce.

# CHAPTER ELEVEN

**Some things are too important to be taken seriously.**

−OSCAR WILDE

"The promposal is today. Today is the promposal" was what I whispered under my breath like a serial killer as I tried to weigh the merits of my purple sundress over my green overall skirt. On the one hand, the green overall skirt sometimes made me feel like a DIY Girl Scout. On the other hand, once I was wearing my purple sundress when a pigeon pooped on my head and Algie was convinced it was because the color somehow influenced the bird's choice of restroom. There were at least a million YouTube videos to help you stylize and accessorize, but none seemed to be titled "What to Wear When You're Putting It All on the Line for Love and You're Also Dressing for Early Spring's Weird Hot/Cold Flashes." And I had googled it, just to make sure.

I decided on the purple sundress. Lightning doesn't strike twice, right?

I checked my phone, and there was a text from Gwen.

Want to hang out later?

I paused. Was not mentioning that we would actually be hanging out later and she just didn't know it yet a lie of omission?

"What were you thinking?" I typed.

Bug movie?

I sat down on the bed. Would the prospect of kissing Gwen ever not threaten to send me to the floor with a not unpleasant loss of control over my legs? I knew historians had basically confirmed that all the swooning women in Victorian times were actually keeling over not because of their fragile female constitution, but because their corsets were cutting off their oxygen supply. But maybe they all just had leg-liquefying crushes?

Let's make it a double feature.

An hour later I sat on a park bench trying not to look at what seemed to me like a conspicuous number of people in dresses and suits for a Sunday morning in the park. I continued to sit on the bench, inspecting my fingernails, which I had painted a matte deep blue last night and had somehow made the journey from my apartment through the park without chipping. I took this as a sign. Another sign: two encouraging texts from Sandra and Emily. A simple "Good luck" from Emily buzzed first, followed by a very long interpretation of my horoscope (sun and star signs) that I skimmed before hitting the TL;DR — this was an excellent day for a promposal. There were no screaming kids in sight to possibly throw off the AMDA kids, who, according to Algie, had just, just gotten the timing right. I took this as another sign. I started singing "I Saw the Sign" under my breath, which was just a sign that I was going to fully lose it if Gwen and Algie didn't show up soon. Cecil was on the other side of the fountain, acting as a "general lookout and observer and source of distant but strong moral support," according to his last text.

"Janey, hey" I heard, and looked up, and there was Gwen, dressed in pale pink skinny jeans and a white button-down blouse with a pale pink sweater. She looked amazing, which I would have figured I'd stop being surprised about by now, but I hadn't. Algie was right next to her, but he quickly took a left and started speed walking in the other direction. I think he thought he was being stealthy, but he just looked like he realized he really, really had to pee.

"Okay, so I guess Algie doesn't want to hang out anymore. Cool," Gwen said, watching him disappear before turning to me and smiling, "But I'm pretty happy with the swap in company."

I smiled, and while I was aiming for something sexy or witty, all I could think to whisper was "So, uh, do you like *Enchanted*?"

Before she could respond, I grabbed her hand and took her toward the fountain, just passing the first carved angel face, our signal that the promposal was a go. The three portable speakers we'd stationed around the fountain growled to life and the dancers were dancing, and I didn't know if they were in time or not because my heartbeat was going a lot faster than 4/4 and that was all I could hear. I couldn't look at Gwen. I wanted to look at Gwen, but I couldn't. I focused on one of the dancers, Benny, who'd never quite gotten the hang of the skip step and looked like he was permanently on the edge of tipping over. The dancers looked amazing as a group, and it was only when I focused in on one or the other that I even could tell they weren't professionals but a bunch of teenagers still dreaming of their first spot on *NCIS*. The music swelled, and I watched Becky and Ryan, who had been tasked with unveiling the banner, move toward the bench, holding the banner rolled up between them. And then, perfectly in time, they unfurled it, and the message and intention of the flash mob became very clear to anyone watching, which included Gwen, who I was still not looking at when I felt her hand close around mine. I waited. Then waited a little more. Then, when I couldn't stand waiting another second:

"Uh, Gwen. Not to pressure you, or rush you, or anything. But . . . the question. It's posed to you . . ."

"You're going to make me say it?" she asked, dropping my hand but dragging her thumb down the side. She turned toward me and took both my hands in hers, a gesture that was so ripped out of one of my favorite Austen movies I could practically feel the skirt of my dress lengthening and blowing in the breeze off a moor.

"I know I hide it well, but I'm kind of a walking collection of insecurities in the shape of a human, and in order not to dissolve, I occasionally need verbal reassurance," I admitted, smiling.

"I would love to go to prom with you. And while we're making things very official, and very musical, I'm not sure how you guys do it at public school, but at the academy, after you hook up in your second bug-themed movie, you're officially a couple," she said.

I couldn't breathe. I could breathe. Breathing felt wonderful. I felt wonderful.

"We're going to our second bug movie."

"Yes."

"So after that, I guess we'll be official."

"I think so."

"Which means, if we were going to put labels on it, that if, like, we ran into someone and I had — I wanted — I would want to introduce you, I could say this is Gwen, my —"

"Girlfriend."

I made sure to complete my cinematic fantasy by brushing a wind-tossed curl behind her ear before wrapping my arms around her neck and putting my lips on hers. And, yes, my just-chipped nail polish caught on her hair, so I was still kind of attached to her bangs as we made out in front of a now cheering crowd of theater students. And a horse clomped by bringing with it that horrific horse smell, and without the music, the blast of car horns could be heard clearly through the trees. But I wouldn't have changed a single detail for anything. I am a Worthing. Sometimes we sit around with barbecue sauce stains on our thighs. But we always, always get the girl.

## GWENDOLYN FAIRFAX, THIRD OF HER NAME, LAST OF HER TAX BRACKET

Gwendolyn Fairfax the Third was born into a life of luxury in suburban Connecticut, something she had no say in but enjoyed well enough for her first few years at least. Educated at the Stanford Day School, followed by Excelsior Academy, followed by Sarah Lawrence College, she went on to become one of Manhattan's most respected social workers, shouldering a towering case load with compassion and beautifully detailed bullet journals.

At the age of twenty-five, with the maturation of her trust, she inherited the largest chunk of the Fairfax fortune, which was left to her by her paternal grandfather, and used it to create a collaborative trust for teens who age out of the foster care system without finding a permanent home.

She lives with her wife, about whom we have not found many identifying details at this time. We are prepared to describe her, however, as some kind of former viral internet star, though as our readers know, that dubious distinction can now be used to label one in four Americans (and an even higher percentage of Canadians!). Ms. Fairfax and her wife were married in the Strand's Rare Books Room. Their first dance: "How Do You Know," from the Disney film *Enchanted.*

# CHAPTER TWELVE

**"You prefer to be natural?"**
**"Sometimes. But it is such a very difficult pose to keep up."**
—OSCAR WILDE, *AN IDEAL HUSBAND*

"You do know prom is in two hours, right? I'm an amazing stylist, but I am still bound by the rules of time and space," Algie said when he walked into my room and took in what I was sure looked like a horrifying lack of preparation. My dress was still laid out on my bed, a beautiful, satiny, gold gown with a slit down the side that Cecil said made me look like a rising star on a late-'90s red carpet. Algie said it looked like an unnecessarily sexy Halloween costume of the golden ticket in *Charlie and the Chocolate Factory*. My hair was not done, though I had applied snail gel under-eye masks that kept sliding down onto my cheeks so that by the time Algie came in, I looked like a football player trying to be nonconformist by wearing white cheek streaks instead of black ones.

"Drink this," he said, holding out one of the two glasses of green juice I was pretty sure he had gotten from Dad on the way up. I watched as a bit of something lumpy floated to the top like a blob in a lava lamp.

"I will not."

"It has, like, every single thing that's supposed to give you glowing skin in it."

"I would rather have dull, lifeless skin and drink a Coke."

"You are hopeless."

"You and my dad are the modern-day victims of a snake oil salesman."

"When they find out my snake oil completely prevents crow's feet, you're going to be jealous," Algie scoffed, putting the glasses down on my bedside table and coming over to peel off my snail masks, rubbing the last of the oily goop into the skin under my eyes.

"Can we please, please start if not the most important, then certainly the most photographed night of our lives?" Algie asked, looking at me with a combination of exasperation and excitement. I nodded, and he ran over to the garment bag I'd laid out next to my dress, unzipping it to reveal his tux, which he'd refused even to send me a picture of, saying it would lessen the impact of the reveal. And maybe he was right, because I was completely in awe of the jet-black material that also somehow had a shimmery sheen, like a piece of obsidian. It looked like I imagined a suit would look if it was enchanted, or really, if it was on a supernatural-themed show and the production team wanted to let the audience know it was enchanted, letting off a soft glow of magic the other characters can't feel but can sense.

"It's perfect, right?" Algie looked to me for actual confirmation of its perfection. I nodded.

"So you and Cecil . . ." I began, letting the pairing hang in the air as I turned toward my shoebox full of makeup, which was mostly free samples and tubes of bright purples and deep blues I'd bought for various Halloween costumes, hoping there was something vaguely lip colored I could put on.

"Cecil and I what?" Algie asked from behind the room divider, where he was putting on his magical tux.

"So are you, like, dating, or officially a couple? I mean, I think he really likes you, and NYU is only a thirty-minute subway ride from his apartment . . ." I trailed off again, not sure how much to reveal.

"Cecil is thoroughly adorable and will make an excellent prom date," Algie insisted in his most pretentious, "interview for an internship with my father's law firm" voice.

"Algie, seriously, stop. If this is just a one-night-only"—I paused for a second so Algie could sing a few lines of the disco version of the *Dream Girls* song—"if this is just a one-night-only thing, Cecil should know that going in. I think it might be, like, romantic imprinting. Like, if he sees your face while slow dancing and 'My Heart Will Go On' comes on, he'll think you're his one true love, no matter how many people try to convince him otherwise."

"They're not going to play 'My Heart Will Go On.' And I'm not responsible for the adoration of others. My beauty and grace are gifts of genetics, and if people get off in court for genetic predispositions, then I should get off for any broken hearts I cause."

"Algie. Serious for a second? He's my little baby cousin. You know I'm always in your corner. But this time I might have to be, like, the loyal whistleblower. Like, I've dedicated my life to this company, but the chemicals are turning all the babies purple, and I just have to say something."

"God, your Netflix binges are getting weirder. Straight talk?

Except, you know, not"—Algie came out from behind the divider mid-sentence, still wearing his jeans but in a white tux shirt—"yesterday we talked for hours. And I don't mean we talked and then got a snack, or we talked and then there was a video I just had to show him, or we talked and made out then talked. He came over around noon, and we stopped talking when I was like, 'What the hell, am I going blind?' And, no, the sun was going down. We talked from light to dark. And I didn't get bored for a minute. My mom came in in this panicked rush because she found my phone on the counter and it was so lit up with notifications, she thought for sure I had been murdered or something. Cecil is not just a prom date. I might have done the NYU-to-his-place calculations too. Which is not something I'm ready to admit to anyone yet. Including Cecil. And, kind of, myself. But you're right. You should know."

"Aw, Algie, have you become a romantic? Are you going to watch YouTube proposal videos with me now?"

"Not in a million years, Janey."

"Do you want me to help you tie your tie?"

"Do you know how to tie a tie?"

"No. But I feel like it's a best-friend duty I should perform. I could look it up."

"I'm perfectly capable of tying my own tie, thank you," he said, tapping something on his phone and then tossing it on the bed as some cheesy '80s pop song played out of the tiny phone speakers.

"We couldn't listen to something from this decade?" I asked.

"We are about to live a fashion montage. A blur of prepping and preening. We need montage music. Now, if you love me at all, you'll plug in your flat iron and let me drive."

Forty-five minutes later, my hair was straight and my cheek bones, forehead, and for some reason I will never understand, the tip of my nose were all vaguely shimmery, and standing in front of the full-length mirror on the back of my door, I looked . . . not like myself. Or at least I looked like a very airbrushed version of myself. Algie stood beside me, and we were both looking at ourselves and each other and the two of us together in the mirror — shiny, hair-sprayed people about to meet up with people who liked us even when we weren't nearly this well put together. I let out a breath. Possibly all the breaths I had been holding in since the beginning of high school. I didn't know I could even feel this happy.

"This is cruel, you know. It's mean to show up to prom looking so painfully attractive the entire student body knows, in an instant, that no matter what Insta filter they use, their social media selves will never live up to our actual selves. Seriously, Janey, we should look at this as a moral question. Is it really right to look this good? I'm pretty sure I could build up a fake zit or two with a little foundation and lipstick. Should we tone things down, for the good of our fellow man?" Algie asked.

"You would never wear a fake zit to prom."

"Well, no, not me, but I thought you might be willing to boost the morale of our graduating class."

"Not a chance."

"Then I guess it's time to go," he said, extending an arm, which I took and linked my arm into as we walked down the hall. We hadn't even hit the bottom step when the flash of my dad's ridiculous ancient Polaroid camera blinded us. Even though Mom had gotten him more than one digital camera and even some add-on lenses for his phone, he always insisted on hauling out the Polaroid he inherited from Grandma whenever he deemed something a momentous occasion because, according to him, "photographs were never meant to last forever like those files on your phone. If you think they'll never fade, you don't work as hard to keep your memories from fading."

"You two look absolutely beautiful," my mom said as she gave Dad a side hug, staring at us with what I hoped weren't, but kind of suspected were, tears in her eyes.

"They look like they could be on one of those CW shows, which troubles me. Janey, Algernon, I need you to promise me you aren't going to become creatures of the night or get involved in any elaborate murder plots or — and I know this one doesn't sound too bad, but just to be safe — avoid looking across a room while some kind of pop punk plays. That can be when the real trouble starts," Dad said, his face still hidden behind the camera. Dad had always insisted on watching my favorite shows with me as quality father-daughter bonding time, which meant he could edit the Wikipedia entries of most teen dramas better than your average sixteen-year-old.

"Yes, sir, Mr. Worthing. We also promise not to get into any shenanigans or tomfoolery," Algie said, tipping his top hat to my dad.

"Glad to hear it. So, when are your dates getting—" He was interrupted mid-sentence by the doorbell. Algie and I grabbed and squeezed each other's hands at the same second, the first time in our entire friendship that the frantic pulse of my nerves was echoed by an equally fast beat of his.

Dad opened the door, and there was Cecil, wearing a black suit I was pretty sure he'd worn to his confirmation but that was nicely accessorized with a deep blue cummerbund and bowtie. He kind of looked like he was about to sing in a middle school concert choir, but his face was glowing so brightly, I swore I could hear the faint hum of fluorescent lights as he looked at Algie. I took a quick look at Algie, who was trying very, very hard to keep his own face vaguely aloof, and was failing miserably. He gave my hand one last bone-crushing squeeze and then leapt to the bottom step, placed his hat on Cecil's head muttering something about completing the look, and kissed him fiercely, a moment my no–personal boundaries father, of course, captured with another blinding camera flash. I was so busy watching Cecil carefully arrange his deep violet flower in Algie's buttonhole, I didn't notice Gwen standing in the doorway until my mom called my name and I looked toward her.

Gwen's hair was half down, with the other half of her brown curls swept up with a silver and gold jeweled clip that made her look like a '50s movie star. Her face was absolutely glitter free and almost completely bare except for bright red lipstick that made me feel pulled to her like a bug to a zapper. Her dress was pure white with blue beading around the waist and strapless. There were suddenly a million things I wanted to do and say, but none of them in front of my parents, so I settled for jumping to the landing and then unintentionally falling into her arms when I tipped forward, having forgotten that my clingy dress would limit my range of motion. She grasped my arm to steady me but also so she could whisper in my ear.

"I got you, Jane."

It was a simple sentiment. Not even terribly original. Definitely not something that should have been able to fill my limbs with helium, lifting me up, up, up, without me even worrying that I was climbing dangerously high. I didn't have to worry. Because Gwen had me.

I managed to come back down and straighten out my dress so I could stand in front of the door, next to Algie and Cecil with my arm around Gwen's waist, as my parents snapped picture after picture in film and digital, flashes punctuating their always-contradicting directions to move a little to the right, no, maybe to the left. Once Dad ran out of film and Mom ran out of pose suggestions, we hugged them and promised again not to drink or do anything else we wouldn't think of doing if we weren't in formal wear. Dad reminded me I still had a two a.m. curfew, and Mom reminded me how dangerous walking down the subway steps in heels can be, and they both reminded me that even though I was going to miss them like crazy in the fall, it might be nice to have a couple of months without quite so many reminders.

Algie and I had struck an agreement: Lyft to the prom and subway back. Algie was horrified by the prospect of showing up to prom covered, or even lightly dusted, in the many substances that have been known to coat the subway. But I had this memory—I didn't even know exactly how old I was, before middle school, I thought—of sitting next to Mom on the L train when a clump of the most sparkly, glamorous people I had ever seen bumped and giggled their way onto the train just before the doors closed. I'd been sure they were celebrities, but Mom just smiled and told me they must be on their way to prom. And I remembered watching everyone sitting around us smiling as they watched the group, a wave of grins spreading from one end of the train to the other in a way I had never seen on public transportation. Algie might have thought walking into the event hall would be our big moment, but I knew getting on the subway after prom was when we'd truly be in the spotlight, and for once, I was looking forward to standing in that circle of light.

Algie must have ordered the Lyft while I was distracted by Gwen, because by the time we got down the steps, an enormous black SUV with two backseats was idling by the curb. Algie slid into the middle row, followed by Cecil. I slid into the back, followed by Gwen. I had barely put my seat buckle on when Gwen's fingers interlaced with mine again. The Lyft driver pulled out onto the road and turned up the music, something wordless and pulsing that became a kind of wall between the seats. Cecil and Algie huddled in their own little cone of silence, Gwen and I in ours. I knew I was risking the up-do Algie had worked so hard on, but I put my head on Gwen's shoulder anyway. She squeezed my hand, then turned toward me just a little bit. The ride was amazing because of, in a weird way, just how ordinary it was all starting to seem. I knew Gwen liked me. Hell, I could even understand why she liked me. I was pretty likable. And that revelation alone was almost bigger than the sight of our fingers interlaced on the shiny silk of her dress.

Then we were there, and after Gwen and me then Algie and Cecil climbed out, Gwen waved them on. They both looked at me, questioningly, like they wanted to make sure I was choosing this particular moment instead of a grand prom entrance with them. I smiled in their direction and nodded. I appreciated being thought of, protectively, even in that small sort of way. But standing there with Gwen was a decision I was happy to make.

"I don't know if this is the right moment, but I thought I should tell you I think I might be falling a little in love with you," Gwen said, her eyes shining, the orange glow from the giant Dunkin' Donuts sign next door doing nothing to dim the radiance of her face.

I felt like I had to dig through a giant pile of words to get to those glorious four—*in love with you*—and as much as I wanted to focus on them, and return them without qualifiers, I knew I also had to push for clarity. Gently push.

"That's a lot of hedging," I whispered.

"Well, I did grow up with my mother. It's possible my emotional intelligence is irreparably damaged," she said, with a little laugh.

It's incredibly jarring to find out you missed a moment that caused you to split in two: your past self and your present self. Past Janey would have let it go. Past Janey was used to ambiguity and infinite questions without an end in sight and a story with no ties to a beginning. Past Janey was in love with the idea of Gwen, which was a lot easier to accept excuses from. Present, current, "coming dangerously close to believing prom might just be the best night of her life so far" Janey was a fan of declarative statements. Of clarity. Of saying things that were true not because you weren't scared of what chain reaction they might set off, but because voicing them was more important than any possible consequence.

"I'm in love with you right now. You don't have to say it back. But I wanted you to know. I'm not falling. I fell, and I've already recovered and am sitting comfortably and naturally, completely in love with you."

I could feel my pulse over every inch of my body as I stared at Gwen, heart pounding almost painfully out of terror and of putting myself so far out there, I couldn't see how to claw my way back in a hasty retreat. But just as strong as my fear was surge after surge of affection, the kind I felt sometimes after coming home from vacation and seeing the silhouette of the skyline against a sunset, or when Dad did his absolutely terrible Swedish Chef impression during dinner, or when Algie sent me a text referencing an inside joke so old I had forgotten it. It was a feeling of love so acute it was almost a surprise, and that surprise brought up a whole new wave of emotion. Like, *Oh my god, this is my city, my family, my person, my girlfriend, and I'm so lucky to love them.* It was not a feeling that was dependent on them feeling it back. Or maybe that was just what I convinced myself of as I waited for Gwen to say something.

She put her hand on the side of my face, gently, and kissed me so softly, my stomach dropped to my toes. Light kisses after declarations of love were rejections, kiss-offs. Past Janey apparently was still there, hovering in the background, because I didn't want to look at Gwen, at the pity I knew would be on her face, but I forced myself to meet her gaze. In complete horror, I realized that she was crying.

"Jane, you are so much braver than me," she whispered.

I didn't think I had been called brave since I had made it through a round of booster shots without crying. I hadn't even really felt brave when, on Cecil's suggestion, I once spent almost an hour in my room striking empowering poses and listening to "Fight Song" on repeat.

"I was hedging. And the hedging was lying. I already fell in love with you. In fact—"

She brought her lips close to my ear. The pause went on for three exhalations. Every time her breath tickled my ear, the feeling coupled with the slowly dawning realization of what she had just said made me think every pearl-clutching parent was right—teenagers were sex-crazed animals—because I wanted nothing more on this earth than to rip off Gwen's beautiful gown right there on that street that smelled like trash and stale coffee.

"In fact—" Gwen started again, "I've fallen, and I can't get up."

She pulled back so I could take in her grin, so brilliant, so pleased with herself that she had punctured a perfectly romantic moment with a reference to that ridiculous Life Alert infomercial–turned-meme Algie loved to text. But she hadn't really punctured it at all. It just triggered another wave, swelling then crashing as I pulled her toward me like we made out in the middle of a busy sidewalk every day.

"Gwen, would you like to enter prom with me?" I asked, offering my bent arm.

"I would, without any hedging, absolutely love to," she said, and hooking her arm within mine, we walked toward the door, two girls who were scared and brave and had decided, independently and together, that it would be better to face those warring emotions with someone next to you, holding your hand.

I had always thought my curfew was pretty reasonable, but in the moment, having a predetermined cutoff time for the best night of my life seemed kind of wrong. But there was really no concise way to explain that to your parents through text. So at 1:30 a.m., after slow dances and fast dances and the kind of dances that are mostly just rhythmic hopping, the four of us carefully climbed down the subway stairs and got onto the train in our formal wear.

As soon as we sat down, we became the human equivalent of tangled earbud cords — Gwen's arm wrapped around my waist, Algie's head in her lap, Cecil's in mine, both of their arms hanging off the bench to let their fingers intertwine, my hand on Algie's shoulder. Our collective energy and body language communicated, almost audibly, that though 364 days out of the year we were good New Yorker subway riders who always put their bags on their laps, tonight, if anyone asked us to move, they would receive only four of the world's most cutting stares. Just like that day I spotted the prom goers, though, we inspired only smiles from the sleepy masses.

"So, is it official?" I whispered to Algie.

"I have no idea what you're talking about," he said, as Gwen rested her head on my shoulder.

"I do. And we are," Cecil answered, pointing to Algie's elementary school Mathletes pin on his jacket lapel. It was nothing special, but its presence on his jacket meant Algie had thought about what would make him happy, then took some time to search for said thing, and allowed himself to be unabashedly corny, even for a minute. Algie had had flings and hookups and a series of dates with the same guys and even the occasional guy who would call Algie his boyfriend whom Algie wouldn't correct. But instigating a declaration of an actual relationship? That was a first. A first that filled me up with hope and love for both of them, all mixed together so I knew that even if the whole thing flamed out in a month, in the not-too-distant future, they'd still be able to look at our prom pictures and smile.

"Janey! We can double date!" Cecil suddenly shouted, making the couple a bench over stare at us. But they smiled. I smiled back, basking in their recognition of our collective adorableness. Gwen and Algie got off first, Algie whispering something in Cecil's ear as Gwen leaned in to kiss me, somehow timing it perfectly so she got to the door with just enough time to breeze through before it closed.

When I turned to Cecil, he was wearing the same kind of goofy grin I could feel stretched across my own face.

"What did he say?" I asked, crossing my fingers that it wasn't too graphic.

"He said, 'End Act I,'" Cecil said, leaning into me, closing his eyes again in complete happiness.

"And that means what exactly?"

"I'm not one hundred percent sure. A start? The promise of Act II? I've always dreamed my boyfriend would be mysterious," he said.

I closed my eyes too, replaying tonight's greatest hits over and over again. Sometimes people change. They become more committed, or more willing to put someone else first, if they really care about them. Not everyone can. Or maybe everyone can, but not all the time. But I think we owe it to each other, sometimes, to give people the space to try.

# CHAPTER THIRTEEN

Life is not complex. We are complex. Life is simple, and the simple thing is the right thing.

—OSCAR WILDE

I half expected Mom and Dad to be waiting up in the dark, ready to hear all the details of prom, but when I got in, the downstairs was quiet, dark, and empty. There was a Post-it Note on the kitchen table next to a chocolate cupcake that read, "In case prom food is anything like wedding food and you need a little extra sustenance — Mom," and underneath in Dad's handwriting, "There's also some unsweetened almond paste in the cabinet, which will actually give you sustenance."

I grabbed the cupcake and started unwrapping it on the way upstairs.

I sat in the middle of my room eating the cupcake for a second, letting the sugar coat my tongue, imagining the good-night text from Gwen I'd find when I pulled out my phone. I imagined good-night texts stretching the length of the summer and into the fall, when we'd be separated by barely more distance than we were now. I finished the cupcake and lay back on the floor. I saw my box of obits sticking out from underneath my bed and pulled it out but didn't open it. Algie always asked if I ever thought about writing mine. I had never put it on paper, but I was constantly writing it, in my head, every time I had a fantasy of the future or made a choice and wondered what it would change, how it would be remembered. I had made the mistake of telling my guidance counselor about the obits once. Ms. Gecko was genuinely sweet and it wasn't crazy of her to suggest the living obits meant I should be a profile writer, or even a documentarian following cool people around. But they weren't what I wanted to share with the world; they were a way for me to understand it.

My phone chimed and I looked down. It wasn't a message from Gwen, but a text from Sandra asking, "How was prom?! I want pics!" As I looked for the best one to send her (it was always really, really tough to pick the best picture of Gwen, who in some photos looked like a celestial being and in others looked like a spokeswoman for Neutrogena), another message popped up, from Emily. "Hope you had a great prom! Looking forward to seeing you next weekend." I had barely typed a reply when I got another, from Cecil (a link to a Spotify playlist that started with "Hopelessly Devoted"), then a string from Algie that seemed to be links to medical journal articles describing instances of people literally dying from a broken heart, which I took to be encouraging, since it confirmed he should be afraid his heart was in danger. I had never been so popular. I had just sent off a heart to Cecil, half a dozen photos to Sandra, and a link to a coupon for fish oil pills (for a healthy heart!) to Algie when a message from Gwen popped up.

> Just so you have it in writing — I love you.

And then I did what I could not in front of Gwen, or on the subway — I stood up, flung my arms out to the side, and let out a completely cartoonishly lovesick sigh as I fell onto my bed, bouncing more than a couple Pound Puppies to the floor.

My phone chimed again, and I slid off the bed to read a new text from Gwen.

> Hey, so I was looking some stuff up, and I found this . . . I don't want to push like Algie, but I just wanted you to know, I'd go with you . . . if you want to try . . .

I clicked on the link to an article about a support group in Brooklyn that helped people track down their birth families. Even scanning through it, I thought it looked more like people who knew their way around adoption agency files and less like people who were ready to become PIs to track down virtual ghosts. But I loved Gwen for thinking of me. I loved Gwen for innumerable things, but that was the one that stood out in that moment. I tapped the edge of my phone, not sure what to reply. I could check it out. It could lead to more answers. More clarity. It could just be an adventure with someone I loved. Someone who got me. Who would be there to steady me.

I put my phone on the floor and opened the obit box. It was almost filled with loose leaf paper, a few typed-up pieces, one on a Post-it Note, and one on the back of a receipt. I pulled out a blank page, or one that was almost blank except for a little I had written years and years ago. My phone continued to chime, creating lines that tied me to people in different cities and different states, who kept me company in the middle of the night. My fingers were still sticky with bits of cupcake crumbs my mother had baked especially for me. They smudged onto the paper a little bit as I wrote, but I didn't mind.

---

## MAYBE HIM, PERHAPS HER, BIOLOGICAL PARENTS OF BAG BABY BABE

They're not together anymore. Or maybe they are. They think of her every day. Or they have to keep her out of their thoughts, because it hurts too much. Or they barely have any memory of her at all, because memories of those years are hazy now, for so many reasons. Today they will wake up and stretch and walk to the bathroom and brush their teeth, most likely. After the tooth brushing, the possibilities seem endless. Maybe not for them, but for the author of their imaginary lives. The kid who they left is a lot taller, with a bigger vocabulary, but has similar feelings about being woken up from a nap. She wonders, but she doesn't yearn. Her life is too full to let the hole get too big. But that will sometimes feel like a temporary state, and she will lie awake wondering if her life were too empty, or not empty but thin, whether the hole would get bigger and bigger and begin to eat away at her, the way an unfilled cavity can. But most of the time she won't worry about that. She'll be able to sit in her room and feel safe and loved, safe and loved enough to think about maybe her, perhaps him, and smile. She can imagine a future when they are found and they come to dinners with all the other people in her life. She can imagine a future when they exist only on this piece of paper. She does not believe, in this moment, in all the powers and forces her cousins Cecil and Sandra believe would be able to get them a message without the use of the internet or the postal service or a carrier pigeon. But she pretends for a moment that she does. She closes her eyes, and sends them a message. *I hope you're okay. I'm okay. I'm better than okay. I hope you know that, too.*

# ACKNOWLEDGMENTS

Thank you to my agent Uwe Stender, who has believed in and championed my work for so many years, and has waded through many, many typos. Thank you to my agent Elle Thompson, who has made this manuscript better in so many ways and has always been so supportive and patient. Thank you to my editor, Lily Kessinger, for seeing something in this story, for turning me into an author.

To Kosoko Jackson, who helped me see this book in a new light. To Sarah Maxwell, for creating a beautiful cover. To Emily Andrukaitis, for making the copy so much clearer and crisper. To the world's best English teachers, Mary Gadd and Mary Collins, who told me I could be a writer, then taught me how.

And to my mother, for listening as I read through every draft, who was there to talk me through every rejection, and who, when I worried that this book might never be published, was always there to ask who they were going to cast in the movie version.